FOR THE SAKE OF SOUL

Fred's stories have a way of catching you off-guard, leading you through unexpected emotions, channels of memory you were sure you'd put away. Instead, the intense accuracy of the experiences and emotions he crafts leaves you needing to read and re-read the stories if only to prove to yourself that the experience was not your own and was truly written on the page. Good stories laden with crafted wickedness that lingers and taunts.

    Kae Sable, author, *Compass for a Host of Sparrows*

Frederick Foote's stories are often provocative and always well worth the read. They at times inspire the reader with a true sense of trepidation that is always rewarded at the end. He is an original, innovative author who deserves a place on your shelf.

    Elaine Zentner, Coordinator, Sacramento Prose and Poetry Meetup

Some of these stories have already been published, but more significantly, the collection is first rate. They kind of remind me of Earnest Gaines' short stories - community and culturally oriented and real life situations contained within a certain era and genre.

    Margaret Washington, PhD, author of *Sojourner Truth's America*.

Also by Frederick K. Foote

"Hana," Akashic Books, 2014

"I Saw the Devil," Specter Magazine, 2014

"The Mechanic," Piker Press, 2014

"Alley Ways," Piker Press, 2014

"Nina," Piker Press, 2014

"Covenants," Aphelion Webzine, 2014

"Thugs," Military Experience and the Arts, 2015

"Southern Grace," Military Experience and the Arts,   2015

"Dreams in Black and White," Sillytree, 2015

"Usama," Piker Press, 2015

"Bone Yard," The Birds We Piled Loosely, 2015

"Wind Song," Short Fiction Break, 2015

"Rocket Eighty-Eight Blues," Sirenzine, 2015

"Crossroads," The Fable online, 2015

"Out of Order," so glad is my heart, 2015

"Blue Black," 82 Review, 2015

Acknowledgments

I must, first of all, acknowledge my wife, Ruth's, encouragement and support in my pursuing this time-consuming craft. I thank you for your patience and understanding.

Our daughter's Zenobia and Zora have taken time from their busy lives to respond to request for comments on my work. I appreciate your time and insights.

Our grandson, Kenneth, has been an avid reader and promoter of my stories.

From my first story to my most recent my granddaughter, Roze has been my most excellent proofer and critic at large. Thank you again for all your help with and interest in my writing.

Dr. Travis Silcox at Sacramento City College introduced me to the art of writing short stories and encouraged me to publish and polish my craft. I'm forever in your debt.

Mr. Mensah Demary published my first two stories in "Specter Magazine" and steered me to tools that have helped me expand my publishing opportunities. Your support has been invaluable.

My MeetUp group, Sacramento Prose and Poetry, is my sounding board and a major part of my writing community. I thank all the members of SPP, including but not limited to: Kae Sable, Elaine Zentner, Regnal Otto, Doug Huse, Jack Ratliff, Julie Howard, Lee Caldarella-Wong, Carol Smiles and our talented and gracious leader Sara Winston.

My special editors were Chez Colson and Enaj Leotaud who made every editing session a laughing matter.

Margaret Washington also took time from her very busy schedule to read this manuscript and provide invaluable suggestions and critiques.

And special thanks to my editor and friend Dr. David Covin for his editorial and critical skills.

I also must acknowledge all the fellow students, family, fellow writers, and friends too numerous to name who encouraged and inspired me.

Copyright by Frederick K. Foote, Jr. 2014 All rights reserved.
Library of Congress in Publication data.

Foote, Frederick R., 1943
For the Sake of Soul

An earlier version of "Litter Wagon," was published by Every Day Fiction, published with permission; an Earlier version of "Guest in Black in White," was published by Akashic Books, published with permission; an earlier version of "Firefight," was published by The Birds We Piled Loosely, published with permission; an earlier version of "The Platform," was published by the Cooper Street Journal, published with permission; "Dead End," was published by Sussurus, published with permission, 2015; "Court Martial of Samuel James Wilson," Second Place Winner, New Voices Contest, published by *Elephant Magazine*, 2015.

1. Blacks in the military 2.Viet Nam War 3. Blacks in the work place 4. Black males coming of age 5. Blacks in mid-century South Carolina 6. Fiction

ISBN - 978-0-9844350-6-7

Published by Blue Nile Press PO Box 188213
Sacramento CA 95818-8213

Publication date 2015

Manufactured in the United States of America

Table of Contents

Prologue	i
FAMILY	1
Guest in Black and White	3
Russell Recalls	6
Running Down	15
Dead End	31
Black and Blue	32
Homeward Bound	34
WAR HERE ... AND THERE	45
The Platform	47
War Stories	52
A Tale of Two Sergeants	54
Firefight	68
Court Martial of Samuel James Wilson	72
Litter Wagon	83
The Home Front	85
GAINFUL EMPLOYMENT	91
The Appointment	93
The Hearing	105

Prologue

You are about to enter Frederick Foote's world. He's a gentle guide, but it's a fierce world. Frederick's stories chart the geography of the African-American experience of his generation, tracing the uprootedness of the Black migration and the groundedness of characters who stake their claims. His protagonists are buffeted by the currents of Jim Crow, war, and discrimination, but these men and women retain their personhood and amazingly, thankfully, their sense of humor.

The story "Guest in Black and White" frames the book and calls upon the ancestors to be with us as we read. Like a chant to the Yoruba deity, Elegua, the story opens the door to what is to come, reminding us of what has been at stake for Black men, and allowing the wisdom of the grandfathers to guide us.

William Faulkner's Yoknapatawpha County has nothing on Fred Foote's Sumter, South Carolina. This is the deep background setting for the "Andrew" stories in this collection. It is a place where mules and men kick back when beaten. Sumter is the place of secrets and the wellspring of both pain and family connectedness. Travel there to see the same story through multiple perspectives, one of Frederick's authorial obsessions, to discover that the truth is elusive and situated in our faulty and self-protective memories.

Next, we move forward to a cluster of enlistment stories, as young men, full of the wildness of their age, are lured by the promise of the military to travel, to escape, and to participate in the great American tableau of war at home and abroad.

When our characters Teofilo and his buddies are off duty in North Philly, they jostle for a place to experience manhood and friendship. And when they must fight, they do so in all the theatres of combat of Frederick's times: Korea, Vietnam, and the homefront. These are stories of bloodletting, standoffs, and uneasy homecomings.

The world of work for the "young, gifted, and Black" generation holds out terrible irony. Stories like "The Appointment"—written with the gimlet eye of someone who's been there—take us into the landscape of affirmative action, where opportunities come laced with land mines.

These are stories of powerful men and women, sexual appetites, the edge of violence, and the cool control of brinkmanship. We can trace the roots of these human drives back into the mythic pasts of the characters and pull the thread through to our contemporary moment.

Unlike a host of other writers of our time, Frederick Foote pens a mature and complex message of race, gender, and the human condition that will draw you in, creep up on you, send you back into the work for affirmation. His warmth and generosity are the sedimentary layers that nurture the unrelenting urgency of these stories. And Frederick's voice is unmistakable: as addictive and potent as a drug.

Are you ready to enter Frederick Foote's world? You have been warned.

Dr. Travis Silcox, PhD

FAMILY

Guest in Black and White

Back in 1949, I lived with my grandparents out in the country on a small farm near Richmond, Virginia. Something serious was going on one day as I entered the kitchen at five-thirty in the morning. Grandpa and Grandma were standing at the sink, staring so intently out the kitchen window, they didn't even hear me come in.

Whatever they were looking at, I wanted in on it. At age six, I was too short to see what caught their eye. I dragged a chair over to the window. The scrape of the chair drew their attention, but just for a second.

They made space for me to stand between them and look down onto the small brook that ran between our house and the slope up to the narrow dirt path that led to the county road.

Grandpa taught by example. He always tried to figure things out for himself before he sought help. I should have waited to see what they looking for, but my curiosity was too great.

"Grandpa, what we looking—"

"Watch the creek by the bushes."

I was bursting to say, "Watch for what?"

I could feel the words trying to worm their way out of my mouth when a colored convict in a black-and-white striped suit slipped out of the bushes, looked around real quick, and sipped water from a cup he formed with his hands. Quick as a bird he disappeared back into the bushes.

"My, oh my, what are we going to do, Matthew?" Grandma asked. "We need to call the Sheriff." She put her arm around me like she was trying to protect me as she talked.

Grandpa was quiet for a while. He returned to his seat and his breakfast. I dragged my chair back to the table and sat down with my grandfather.

"Matthew, he could be a robber or killer or God knows what. We need to call—"

"Hmm, that's true, sure is. And it could be me, or Preston," he nodded at me, "or any other black man in the wrong place at the wrong time."

Grandma looked ready to do something, even if it was wrong. "We got to look out for Preston. That convict is right outside our house."

"We ain't calling nobody."

Breakfast was angry looks from Grandma, and rock still silence from Grandpa.

Grandpa picked up his lunch box and put on his hat. He put his big hand on my shoulder. "Stay close to the house. Listen to your grandmother. Keep your eyes open."

He nodded to Grandma and looked over at the double barrel 12-gauge shotgun over the fireplace. And he was out the door.

We watched him from the kitchen window as he marched down the ridge to the creek. He walked right up to the big rock near where the convict was. My grandpa opened his lunch pail and took out a big slice of our own cured ham, a hunk of cheese, biscuits, and Grandma's special-occasion coconut cake. He put it all on the rock.

He started to turn away, but stopped. He took out his thermos, pulled off the cup, and poured it full to the brim. He left the cup on the rock and walked straight and tall up to the road.

As soon as he was out of sight, the convict was out of the bushes, scooping up the food and burning his mouth on the coffee.

I helped clean up the kitchen, but my mind was on the convict and my grandfather. I wondered if I would ever be as desperate as the convict, or as decent or as wise as my grandfather. It's been sixty years, and I still wonder about that to this very day.

Russell Recalls

Our 1936 Fordson tractor rears up like a horse stung by a wasp, rears up and topples over backward. It falls on my Papa, crushes the life out of him in his own field.

The greedy soil that he watered with his sweat soaked up his fresh blood for dessert.

I'm, in the mule shed. I hear the tractor engine change pitch, hear the... the... thud... there is no screaming...my papa never cried out. It happens that quick...

The, the day, day... before... we, we were talking, talking about the Supreme Court school desegregation cases, Thurgood Marshal, the NAACP... and...

"You got the brains to do that Rusty, but it takes more than brains. It takes guts and a lot of heart."

We're grooming our two mules, Kush and Kemet. Something all four of us enjoy. But I don't want to be a lawyer or judge or preacher or politician. I could never get into that. And it was, was just like Papa was reading my mind, "Rusty, most important be yourself. People be putting a lot of heavy expectations on you, including me, but every man has got to find his own way in life; you hear me?"

All I hear now's the 'thud' like a 10,000-pound sledge hammer pounding the earth. That sound... wakes me in a cold sweat... with a racing heart and fear on my breath... I don't remember that much. I don't, honest... just bits and pieces.

###

I remember... I'm in bed, under the cover, in my clothes with my shoes on. I'm shivering. I can't get warm. I'm so cold. I'm freezing.

The A&E Express, that's what papa calls Andrew and Emma, my favorite cousins, yank the cover off me and Andrew's pulling me up to a sitting position. I call them Mutt and Jeff. Emma's tall for 12 and Andrew's small for 11.

"Russell, Russell you have to go talk to Reverend Grimes and the funeral man. They'll be here any minute now." He shakes me by the collar. "Come on man."

I smile at Andrew and rub his head. I smile at a detached looking Emma standing by the door. I wave at her to get her attention.

Andrew shouts at me, "Get up! You the man of this house now! Get up and act like it."

I try to get back under the covers. Andrew holds on to my collar with one hand and grabs my left ear lobe with the other. He gives my ear a vicious twist. I scream and jerk away from him. I'm standing now, lifting my little cousin off his feet. I'm ready to smash his face in.

He doesn't look scared at all. His voice's deeper than I remember, an odd familiar kinda voice. "Get out there now."

He and Emma each takes an arm and pulls me toward the bedroom door.

"Funeral director? Who died?"

"It doesn't matter. You have to do this for your Papa. He can't do this. He's depending on you." Andrew's voice's back to normal or nearly normal.

I'm in my hallway. They shut the door behind me. Maybe they did. I must be seeing things like the DDTs. My mama can't stand Andrew. She barely lets him in the house. Somebody died… I think- there's a knock on the front door. Front door? Nobody uses the front door.

The white, black woman, with the bright blue eyes and black hair, the woman who don't like anybody around here, much is going to answer the door. She sure didn't care that much for her husband, my father, or me.

I beat my mama to the door. She looks at me like I'm crazy. The same way she looks at me most of the time.

I open the door and invite the funeral director and Reverend Grimes in.

I sit at the head of the dining room table where Papa sits.

Things just pop out of my mouth, "Is his burial insurance going to pay off?" I know that lots of colored people get cheated on their burial insurance. Papa told me about that.

Mr. Norton, the funeral director, goes to hewing and hawing.

I cross to the sideboard and pull out his insurance papers, "It's paid up to date. It better cover everything. And I do mean everything."

Mr. Norton turns to Mama to try and get her to understand the complexities of funerals and all the unanticipated costs.

Mama's furious at me for taking over the meeting, but she'll not undermine me in front of these two, besides, she's pretty tight with a penny.

I don't remember much else... something about his plot... maybe. After a while, I just wanted to get back to my room before Andrew and Emma mess with my things.

When I get back to my room, they're gone. Maybe they were never here, but when I touch my earlobe, it's tender to the touch, and red and angry looking.

I go out to tend to Kush and Kemet. I know who died. I know how he died. So do Kush and Kemet. We know, but we don't talk about it. Not a word.

He told me not to mess with the A&E Express because there's really only one of them sharing two bodies. Sometimes I couldn't tell when he was joking or serious. I miss him. I do.

###

It's all a fog, hazy with blind spots. I do know the A&E Express looked in on me every day. I know that.

I know that I could not have done the funeral without them. I know I wish I was with them tramping through the woods, eating green apples, catching perch and bluegill or sitting in my back yard listening to him talk about Africa and our hidden history, or Bapu Gandhi, or atomic energy, W.E.B. Du Bois, or civil Rights or Gene Debs or Richard Wright.

I think he was talking to all of us. I know we all listened, but I always felt he was trying to make sure Andrew and Shad understood. Shad, Uncle Eddie's oldest son, is fourteen like me. He's a quiet boy. Not shy or scared ... just likes to keep to himself. Why those two? What's so special about them? Emma and I are the scholars, the ones with a bright future.

It's the pity in their eyes I can't stand. I'm like Shad now. I keep to myself, stay around the house, but not in the house. Mama makes that impossible.

"Andrew, how do you get along with Aunt Irene? Do you ever think your mother hates you?"

We're patching the wire on our chicken coop. Emma's down at Uncle Eddies.

The questions cause Andrew to freeze in the act of striking a nail with his hammer. I know he doesn't like talking about his mother. I'm just at loose ends. I don't mean any harm. He lays down the hammer. He turns to face me.

"She's only here once a year for a week... Grandpa says I have to treat her with respect... no matter. I try to do that. He pauses for a long time. "I think she's... is... you know... you know... aaahh, just a little off, you know?"

I can see the pain in his eyes. I can see he loves his mama. I see that. I wish he would see that in my eyes. I look for it in the mirror. I look hard. I can't find it.

I put my hand on his shoulder. He shrugs it off and goes back to nailing. He leaves a little later, walking. Andrew never walks when he can run, even if it's just down past the three houses down the road to Uncle Eddie's.

###

We sold Kush and Kemet, our prize-winning gray mules. Mr. Powers, down the road, bought them. He'll appreciate them. I'm glad for them. I wish I could have gone with them. I could live in a stall in a barn. No pity in their eyes. I could do that.

The last job for the mules was pulling the tractor up to the garage. Shad, the A&E Express, and I, pushed it into the shed. I'm taking it apart, selling the pieces for scrap.

Mama is outraged at my "low life nigger behavior." She believes we could have got "good money" for that twenty-eight-year-old killer tractor. She's so damn greedy.

###

I saw him last night. He was in the back yard talking to Andrew and Shad. Emma was standing behind him. I was outside the circle. I yelled, and screamed, and screamed. They couldn't hear me.

Mama is shaking me. The sweat is flying. I push her away. I run to the backyard, but they are gone.

###

Cheryl keeps coming by. I don't need a girlfriend now. I send her away. She comes back like a bad penny. I take her out to the mule shed. I fuck her. That's what she wants, but she's crying and fighting like crazy. The bitch is crazy. She runs out of the shed half dressed, just acting real crazy.

###

Mama has gone to locking her bedroom door at night. My cousin Millie won't come down here anymore, not even with our boy cousins. Is everyone going crazy?

###

The A&E Express is here. My mama called them in the house, even Andrew. She locked the door after they went in. She despises Andrew. I know she's talking about me, trying to turn them against me. Yeah, fat chance, they're my cousins, my blood. They're on my side.

Andrew tells me to take a bath. Tells me just like that. The world's going crazy? Who the hell does he think he is? Fuck him. Fuck the A&E Express. He uses that voice. It sounds like him... maybe... I think. Goddamn you Andrew.

I take the bath and put on the clothes they have laid out for me. The A&E Express hugs me before they go. They should take me with them. I belong with them. I do.

###

I'm in the garden picking worms off the tomato plants when it comes to me. "He was giving me a hint, trying to tell me. I was too dense to see it. He called them "The A&E Express," not the R&A&E Express or the Russell and Andrew and Emma Express. I'm not part of them. What? But they told me, included me... fooled me... made a fool of me. They just used me. They laughed at me behind my back. Fuck! Goddamn it! Shit!

Emma, that fucking bitch, teased me and then, and then, laughed about it with Andrew. The fucking cunt used me. Goddamn it all to hell.

Andrew put her up to it the skinny little fucker.

Laughing at me taking a bath, oh, they must have got a big kick out of that.

I'm shaking so bad. I have a chill or a thrill, a thrill on the hill chill. I'll fuck Emma up. I'll fuck her up the ass. She'll suck my dick until she chokes on it. She'll pay for that bitch Cheryl's half-assed dick sucking. God I'll make her pay, and I'll make Andrew watch, yeah, yeah, yeah goddamn right.

###

I have to be careful. I have to. I remember what happened to Dodd. I do. Dodd's 16 and Uncle Eddies oldest son, he's always in one kind of trouble or another.

Last year when Emma was here, Dodd got into it with Andrew. I didn't see that part. Shad and Daniel told me about it.

It all happened so quick. Andrew said something, and Dodd was on him like a terrier on a rat. Before Shad or Daniel could intervene, Emma came out of nowhere with a 2x4 in her hands. She hit Dodd so hard he flew off of Andrew. She knocked him out cold. She would have killed him if Andrew hadn't jumped up to stop her.

I didn't see that, but a week later, after Dodd stopped throwing up and sleeping most of his days away, I saw him confront Emma and Andrew.

A half-dozen of us was there. We was there to protect Andrew and Emma. We would be in scalding hot-water trouble if we let a bigger kid really hurt a smaller kid.

At the end of the road, near the Shortcut, Dodd was ready to bash in Emma's face. She told him to do his best, but that he had better kill both of them right now. The A&E Express meant it. We all knew they did.

Dodd backed down. He's tries to hide it, but he's been scared of Emma ever since.

So, I have to be careful. I do. I will be careful. "One person in two bodies." I have to remember that. I do.

###

The stupid bitch, stupid, stupid bitch I have her. I have her! In a hammer lock! I have her face bent to the floor of the mule shed. Her face in the shit! I have her arm twisted up near her neck.

Oh yeah! Yeah! Just a squeal of surprise, no scream not yet. "Emma! Emma! You gonna do what I tell you. Unbuckle your overalls. Do it bitch!

Don't look at me! Don't even try to look at me. Stupid bitch!"

She's not looking at me. She's looking over in the corner, in the dark corner where the hay is stored.

"Unbutton-"

"Listen." She's clear, she's ... she's like she's not in pain at all.

"FUCK YOU! I will not listen. I-

A rustling in the hay, what... mice that's all... just mice...

"Listen."

I swallow hard. There's nothing, just mice... she's trying to... mess with me... I- there it goes again. What's happening in the hay? "I'm not scared. Come on out. Andrew, is that you? Andrew, get out here now! I will break her arm. I will."

I pull up on her arm. She just gasps a little. She should be screaming.

"Outside, listen, listen he's running, coming here... listen."

"No, no he's in the hay! Shut up bitch. He's in the fucking hay."

Are those thumps outside, bare feet on a dirt road... no... no he's in the hay. He's got to be, got to be... thud, thud, thud... coming from outside or in the hay. I grab the pitchfork. I need to stab the hay... but if he comes through the door... the hay... the door, no, no the hay.

"Emma!" Fuck she's gone, fuck how did she... the hay... the hay! I stab and stab the hay. I must have killed him in the hay. I crawl into the hay looking for the body... "No use hiding now you're dead... like he is... just as fucking dead."

Uncle Eddie, and, and Mr. Jones and Uncle Arnold are helping me out of the hay. Was I sleeping? Why was I sleeping in the hay? Oh, God, I killed Andrew. Oh, no, no… they lead me out to the yard, a police car's in the yard… what happened, oh, oh I killed Andrew- Wait, wait there's Andrew and, and Emma… Oh God, oh God thank, thank God. Thank you Jesus. Thank you lord.

  Handcuffs, handcuffed in the back of the police car. They say I can sleep… they don't mind if I sleep. I need a blanket I'm so cold. Mamas putting a blanket over me, so I can be warm and sleep. I need to sleep so bad. I do.

###

  That was six months ago. I'm better now. I'm so much better. They visit me. Mama, the A&E Express, Uncle Eddie. The doctors say I'm making "wonderful progress" and they're so right. The eyes don't bother me now, no not at all. I don't mind the pity anymore... not at all... in fact, I sneak looks into the eyes and savor the tasty, salty bits of fear in there... yeah I do. It's delicious... delightful. Papa was right, was so right. I just have to be true to myself. I do.

Running Down

It's Saturday morning. He's backed the car out of the garage. He's washed it. It really didn't need it. Now, he's waxing it. He loves that ancient old piece of shit Ford.

He's fifteen now. We've been at this shit for three years. It's been a rough ride on a bumpy road. We both bruised and battered. My fault, it's my fault. I knew better. Eddie told me. Ellen warned me. Annie tried to reason with me. I see it now. I regret my choice. I'm so fucking bullheaded sometimes. I was never meant to be anybody's mother, never. I knew better, but I didn't do better. Now, I've screwed up his life even more. And I still don't understand why I brought him to California. What was I thinking?

The first year I terrified him. I know that now, the death of his grandparents, the abrupt move away from family and a life he loved. It all frightened him. He didn't want to leave South Carolina. And me, all he knew of me was my spiteful ways and short temper. He was scared to death. He tried not to show it, wanted to be a man like his grandfather, strong, silent, no whining, no complaining. Work hard. Pay your way. The old bastard got to him good. Stamped him for life.

The first weekend he was here, he backed that car out. I was about to have a fit. He was twelve years old. I was going to lash into him until I remembered, remembered that he was driving Eddie's tractor at age ten. Me too, at ten we were driving our family tractor, me and Eddie. Our fifteen years before the mast.

The first year was the worst for him, the bed wetting, the night terrors, him crying in his room at night, trying to cry softly so I wouldn't hear. He would barely eat for the first few weeks, that was all my handy work. I have not been a good mother at all. I didn't want to be as bad, as brutal a beast as my father. I have never hit him. At least, I never did that. I've done worse things though. I understand that now. I got good advice from the people I trust most in the world. I disregarded all that and snatched his ass up. I brought him to this place he didn't know, to live with a person he didn't like. Why? Why would I do that? What kind of mother would do that?

He is so tall, sprung up at thirteen. Just shot up, from five-six to five-ten in eight months. Still growing. I worry about him looking older than he is. That could get him hurt, or worse.

Aww, here comes Kiko from across the street, poor little thing. Thirteen and looks like she's ten. She has it so bad for him. So bad it hurts me to watch her sometimes. Kiko, baby, you don't stand a chance. You're too young, too small, and too plain, and that's being generous. I like you. I do, but the project girls got their hooks into him. Baby, he don't even see you except as his friend Alvin's pesky little sister.

I watch her pick up a rag and start waxing. She has strong talented hands. I will say that for her. She's saying something. He's laughing. He's so quiet around here. In our house, no, it's my house. How many times have I made that clear to him? In spoken and unspoken ways.

Speak of the devil, here comes two of them project fiends now. Walking down my street, bouncing their boobs and shaking their asses like they in a parade. One is Isabel, the fifteen year old Mexican slut with a body like Marilyn Monroe, an angel's face and a deep dark desire to hurt and maim. Andrew is dizzy over her, drunk on her looks and the smell of always cooking pussy. And a new girl I don't know. She is black, tall, pretty with a big bust. Jesus Christ, what do they want? Isabel knows she ain't welcome here. She wants something bad to come to my house. Shit, there I go again.

Look at this shit! They ganging up on him. One on each side. Pressing their boobs into his shoulders. Whispering in his ears. Bitches. Something rotten is in the wind.

I step out on the front steps. The girls see me. They intensify and speed up their whispering. I cross to them. Quick. Isabel wants to say something smart. But she got better sense than that. They both move off down the street with some pep in their step. Isabel has jockeyed her way to the street side. She wants to put her friend between me and her. Not a bad idea. "Andrew, I need you today. I need you to go across the river with me."

He didn't even see me coming. They had him fucking enchanted.

He gives me his dead face. No emotion. No anger. No response. Dead to me. "Andrew, do you hear me?"

"When do you want to go?"

That is strange. Not what he said, but how he said it. I think... I think he's glad I intervened. I will hurt them bitches... they just don't know me at all. Out of the corner of my eye, I see Kiko giving the retreating girls the evil eye and the finger with both hands.

"Kiko, ask your Mom if you can go with us."

Kiko lights up like a sunflower. She gives me a smile that makes her, just for a moment, an appealing - almost attractive young girl. She sprints across the street.

He is relieved. His shoulders have relaxed. He rubs both hands on his pant legs. Poor baby. I'll try to keep you safe. I will. I'll send you back to Eddie if that is what it takes. I screwed up so much. I'll not screw this up.

Alvin crosses the street. The boys are immediately involved in a discussion of their comic book project.

Kiko rushes back across the street. She has attempted to rearrange her disaster of a haircut. She has changed into a pink sun dress that does not flatter her tooth pick arms and legs.

Andrew asks if Alvin can come. I say yes. Alvin is delighted. Kiko is crushed. She gives her brother the same look she had recently bestowed on the project girls. If there was a lead pipe handy, I think Alvin would be out cold, or worse, about now.

I feel for her.

So I spend my Saturday afternoon chauffeuring around my son and his Korean friends. I'm glad to do it. I will drive them around every fucking day if it'll keep Andrew safe.

###

I thought the worst was over. We managed through avoidance. We see each other as little as possible. Daylight hours when he is not in school or doing chores or homework, he is out, across the street at Alvin's or around the corner with his project friends.

And in the summer, we both get a break. He goes back to South Carolina. Stays with my brother, Eddie. Gallivants about with my sister, Ellen. She spoils him rotten. And he gets to spend time with his evil, ass cousin, Emma, Ellen's daughter. Emma's his best friend. My son is in deep shit. He is an evil woman magnet. First me. Then Emma. And now this crazy bitch Isabel. Even Ellen can't compensate for all that concentrated female wickedness.

But, these girls out here are so bold. Started calling him at thirteen. Shit, my son is handsome, but he ain't Harry Belafonte. What's going on with girls today? This is 1959. If girls act like that now, what will they be doing next year or the year after? Annie, my Brother Ed's wife, has five boys. I talked to her about it. I thought maybe it was just a California thing. Not so. Even in the back woods of South Carolina where Annie lives, they doing the same shit. She ended up taking the phone off the hook and only using it when she wanted to make a call.

So, even if he had stayed in South Carolina, he would be dealing with this kind of shit, but I don't believe that there is an Isabel in South Carolina. She is one of a kind, a California original. Not normal girl, manipulative, nothing like that. She enjoys other people's pain. She likes it even better when she is the cause of the pain, and she likes it best when she inflicts the pain. Doesn't give a fuck about the boys she wraps around her fingers, or the girls in her court.

She has a grand scheme. She is gathering her pawns and pieces. I don't think she is even aware of what she wants. She is working it out as she goes along. I don't give a fuck about her plans. I just want her to leave Andrew out of them.

And this year, he doesn't want to go home. No home. Isabel got his nose wide open. And she ain't giving him shit. Just playing him. Playing him until she can find a way to use him, or fuck him up for the fun of it. She just don't know who she's dealing with here.

Annie cautions me against trying to break them up. She says that will most likely make things ten times worst. She cautions me about my temper. Her suggestion; learn everything you can about Isabel and about her relationship with Andrew. Hold Andrew as close as you can. That's her advice. I try to follow it.

I think that the day I took the kids across the river was one of the best of days for all of us. After I picked up a few things I didn't need. at the I Street Market, on a whim, I drove us down to Davis to the UC Campus. I parked close to the Quad.

As we crossed the street to the Quad, this tall, blonde, Viking woman came striding toward us. She had to be six feet tall. A full-bodied woman, no more that eighteen or nineteen, but a woman already. She held her books in her right arm, in white shorts and white blouse. She radiated confidence, friendliness and good health. She gave us the brightest smile. A smile for all of us. A smile for each of us. We all turned to watch her walk away.

Alvin punched Andrew in the shoulder, "Andrew, did you see that shit. Man, I can't wait to go to Davis. I'm definitely coming to school here."

Andrew punched him back. "Man! Do you think we could enroll today? She's smoking."

"Andrew, I saw her first. You know I did."

Even Kiko is in awe of the mighty Viking woman.

I want Andrew here. Right then and there, I decide I want him at UC Davis. I want him in this fairy tale town. I don't want him with white girls, but I want him away from the projects. I'm tall. Over five-ten. It's hard to be a tall girl. You get cut out of a lot of things. Hard to find the styles that fit you and the current fad. You can feel awkward and out of step. The boys you really like are always shorter than you. It can work on your mind. Undermine your self-confidence.

The Viking had the confidence that I want Andrew to have. I want him to be comfortable with himself in any surroundings. I want him to smile at strangers like that, a real smile, from the heart. She's probably not a white girl at all. She must be Scandinavian or something.

The more I think about it. I think we may have caused the smile. The boys are happy to be someplace new with each other. Kiko is deliriously happy to be with Andrew. And me, me I'm at peace, contented to see these kids enjoying life and each other.

Shit, we triggered the smile. I bet we did. Fuck, I can do this shit every week. Take them somewhere. I can do this. I can. The possibilities are unlimited. There must be a million places to take them.

We split into pairs. Kiko and Andrew are off to see the cows. Kiko is crazy to see a cow. She is beyond happy. She will have Andrew all to herself for an hour or so. She is a little white tug boat pulling the brown ocean liner across the Quad.

We find the arts buildings. Alvin wants to see if there are any art exhibits. He is comfortable with me. He is chatting away. I have never seen him talk to any adult this much. It hits me like a punch in the stomach. He is more comfortable with me than my own son is. I stumble. I almost fall. He catches my arm, steadies me. A concerned look flashes across his face. I smile. It's an "all's OK" smile. Just a stumble. I'm good. What a lying fucking smile that is.

The halls are full of student art work, some dazzling stuff, Water colors, oils and charcoal and pencil sketches. Alvin is now the tug boat pulling me from drawing to drawing. He has never touched me before, now twice in five minutes. I don't know if I can handle this shit.

A red-headed white woman is removing some drawings and replacing them with others. She has a little cart with her.

Alvin is off to ask her about the drawings. The boy has never been this outgoing. By the time I get there they are having a serious discussion about a drawing she has just put up. The redhead turns to me.

"Hello, I'm Edith Moore. I teach here. I teach art here." She extended her hand to me. She is about five-six, in her late thirties, a few pounds overweight, with large round glasses, green eyes and very long, fine fingers.

"This is Miss Carter. She's my best friend's mother. She's, like, my second mother." Alvin is gushing. I'm blushing. Where is all this shit coming from with Alvin? Moore is smiling at my discomfort, but it is a nice smile.

She takes Alvin on a tour of the building. They chat away like old friends. I follow behind them. We end up in an art classroom. Alvin is drawing for her, at her request. I hope she appreciates his talent. He does have talent. I've seen his work. We stand by the window watching him.

She hits me with a low blow, completely unexpected, a cheap shot, totally uncalled for. "Miss Carter, you must be a wonderful mother. Alvin sure adores you."

I go all pale and weak. What the fuck is going on with me? I excuse myself, Rush to the bathroom, throw up.

She's there a minute later. I'm splashing water on my face. She crosses to me, concern on her face. She touches my shoulder.

Too much fucking touching. I grab her hand. I hold it a bit too long. Hope flares in her eyes, later, later we will talk later. I smile at her as I stretch my legs to get out of this building as soon as I can. Alvin is waiting by the bathroom door. Another fucking concerned face, again.

In the air at last, on the Quad. I feel better. I'll come back later. I'll see Moore. I'll keep my unspoken promise.

Kiko races across the Quad to us. Shows us a bracelet with charms on it, a black-and-white cow, and a UC Davis logo. Andrew bought it for her. To her, it is a friendship, engagement, and wedding ring, all rolled into one.

We walk into town. Eat at an Italian restaurant. We are starved. The food is very good and reasonably priced. Between every other bite, Kiko stops to admire her bracelet.

On the ride back, Kiko falls asleep on Andrew's shoulder. I think this may be one of the happiest days in her whole life.

Alvin actually tells me that this has been one of the best days of his life. He declares, again, that he is on his way to UC Davis to study art and date giant white girls. Moore encouraged him on the art. She doesn't know about the giant white girl thing. He has a goal now. I think he will reach it. That night I can't sleep. I keep replaying our visit to UC Davis over and over.

The Viking. The smiles. The delight the children have in exploring somewhere new, in each other, in life. The touches by Alvin. I want Andrew to touch me like that. To grab my hand like that. I need that. I can say that now. I couldn't say that three years ago. I couldn't. I'm not used to touches. But, but Alvin's touch was not bad. And Moore, maybe I will see more of Moore. I think there is a possibility that I can reclaim my son. I drift off to sleep on that happy thought.

I tell myself I brought Andrew to California because I'm his mother. As a mother, I have the obligation to raise my own child. That's the lie I tell myself. That's a crock of shit. When he was born, I was fourteen and in no position to care for a baby. But I could have picked him up when he was three or four. I had the means to take care of him then, but I left him with my parents. I didn't pick him up until both my parents were dead.

He would have thrived with Annie and Eddie. He gets along well with his cousins. That was the right move. A mother concerned with the best interest of her child would have made that choice. And he could have got by with Ellen. My sister loves Andrew more than she does her own daughter. No matter her circumstances, she would have been overjoyed to have "her" Andrew with her. They have a natural rapport. They always have.

So why bring him here when there were much better places for him?

I do try, and I have some successes. Six months after the trip to UC Davis, we have made three trips - to Berkeley, a pear festival in the Delta, and a Filipino festival in Stockton. I would like to take just the boys, but Kiko would be crushed. I took her on two shopping trips downtown. Just the two of us. I learn she is the brightest of the three by far. I also learn that she is also the most ruthless of the three, maybe of the four, of us. I actually start to worry about what she'll do to Isabel if she ever gets a chance.

Things are better between me and my son. Things are thawing out. It is the best they have been since he has been with me. We watch a new show, Peter Gunn, and I join him watching the Friday night fights. I like the boxing too much. I always have. We bet a quarter, fifty cents, or a chore we do not want to do.

In July, it starts falling apart. He is still "seeing" Isabel. She yo-yo's his life around at will. I bite my tongue.

I have two co-workers that live in the projects. I enlist them to help me keep tabs on what is happening in the projects. One has a son Andrew's age, and another has a daughter a year older.

The news is bad. In August, Isabel is going with a twenty-four-year-old Mexican thug, Miguel Martinez. A vicious punk, disliked by most people in the project, even the other thugs. She still keeps Andrew on a string.

The news gets worse. Isabel - for whatever reason - has decided to drive a white boy out of the projects. She has some of her project "boyfriends" beat him up, twice. After that, they leave him alone. She can't cajole them into whipping him any more. She turns to Miguel. Miguel puts the boy in the hospital with broken ribs and a fractured skull.

September comes as hot as summer.

He misses the Friday night fights. The first fight is just ending. My informant calls. Miguel just caught Andrew leaving the projects headed home, threw him up against the wall, pulled a switchblade on him, and threatened him.

I get the thirty-eight revolver I took from my father. The one I was going to use on my father. I have it in my purse, headed toward the garage when the front door opens.

He has a wild look in his eyes. He doesn't see me. He touches his neck. He looks around. "Hey, where are you?"

I step into the living room. "Where is he? Where is he right now?"

He doesn't know how I know. He doesn't ask. "Please, leave it alone I got it covered. Please." He tries to brush past me. I block him.

"Stay home tomorrow. Stay away from the projects for a while. OK?"

"No!" Loud. Defiant. Scared. "No." Softer almost tenderly. He moves around me. Goes to the bathroom. Goes to bed. Not another word.

I call my informant; tell her he's all right. She is near tears, thankful. She is the one with the boy Andrew's age. I get more information. Miguel has a fifty-six Chevy convertible, blue and white, lowered. He likes to pick up Isabel after school, fucks her, feeds her, takes her home.

I'm parked a half a block from Isabel's unit. I have been here for an hour before they drive up. They park across the street from her place. She has him pinned against the driver's side door. I think she is playing with his dick. They don't see me until too late. She looks up starts to say something.

I open the door. They tumble out.

"Surprise, Surprise." I drop kick her off of him. I hear her rib crack like that breakfast cereal is supposed to sound.

He is on his back trying to get up. I bring the butt of the heavy old thirty-eight down on his right collar bone, an easy bone to break, an attention getter. He falls back down moaning. I slam the pistol into the right side of his face. Something cracks. It's not my thirty-eight that's for sure. I slap his head back the other way, just as hard. I beat him like Louis beat Schmeling. I break his nose. The blood flows. He is almost unconscious.

Her turn now. I take out the two-front upper teeth, and split both lips wide open in one easy move. This fucking gun is better than a hammer. She goes into a fetal position. One stomp, and another rib on the other side snaps. Back to him, he has ribs too.

I don't see the crowd standing back across the street, but I hear them. I know they're there, some watching in revulsion, in fear. Others, I can feel them, loving every minute of it.

I don't see the boy running toward me past the crowd. I sense him. I swing to face him the gun aimed at his chest, at Andrew's chest. He saves his life. One word I have never heard him say in his life to me.

"Mom!"

The rest is hazy. He drives me home, tries to wipe the blood off me, tries to talk to me. He can't reach me. I'm with his grandfather. My father. We are reminiscing about the good old days. What a time we're having.

He's scared the cops will come and take me away. I have terrified him again. No cops. People in the projects don't like to talk to cops. Besides, the cops know Miguel from way back. They put the cuffs on Miguel right away. Beat half to death and they cuff him. They're glad someone "tuned him up." Even if someone told them who it was, they're not interested in arresting anyone. As to Isabel, if she's with Miguel, she had it coming. White cop thinking. White cop thinking saves my black ass. Case closed. Just more nigger shit in the projects.

He's even more of a stranger now. Comes and goes as he pleases. His project friends are lost to him. He has lost interest in the comic strip, in school. I don't know who his friends are now. Sometimes a woman, a full-grown woman, calls here for him. She is always polite, respectful. He still does his chores, faithful to the end.

He tells me one night, about ten, when he comes in. Tells me he helped beat up the white boy the first time.

What the fuck does he want from me? I take another drink of gin. Go to bed.

If he's a stranger. I'm a pariah. My father said I was a loner. I'm a lot more alone now. It's good. I like alone. Shit, I never wanted to be no Eleanor Roosevelt anyway.

All in all, it is some stinky shit, fertilizer for miracles, but no miracle for me.

###

In three years, Kiko has grown from a five-two thirteen-year-old to a five-eight sixteen years old. Grown so fast, she is like Baby Huey, clumsy in her fast-growing body. She looms over her parents and brother.

She has nice legs. With the thickness that black men crave, a respectable ass, for an Oriental girl. Her shoulders, arms, and neck are lovely. She has a bosom that complements her face and upper body. Her face is good with character, strength and bit of charm, especially around Andrew.

The problem is Andrew is not around that much. And when he is, he's moody and closed up. He's never mean to her. He just never really looks at her, like he never looks at me. Far worse than being mean.

She did all of this for him. Grew like that, pledged herself to him that time at UC Davis when we were admiring the blonde Viking woman. She intends to give him what she thinks he wants. I know this in my heart.

Her time is running out. In seven days, he will be in the Air Force. She's desperate. I try to help. We shop, a lovely off the shoulder, simple blue dress, some new white pumps. A flattering short haircut. And, of course, her UC Davis charm bracelet. We put it all together.

Saturday, he's in the driveway, sharpening the lawn mower blades with a file. He is fixing all the little problems around the house, preparing to leave. For good, I think.

She looks good crossing the street. Walks right up to him.

"Andrew, let's go to a movie." A good strong voice. No begging or pleading in it. He barely looks up.

"Naw, not today."

"You'll be gone soon. There are some good movies playing today." A tiny bit of pleading creeps into her speech.

Please hold strong Kiko.

He sighs. Looks at her.

His head jerks back. His eyes open wide.

"You look nice Kiko. Uh, you must have a boyfriend."

My idiot child. My own son. How could he? How dense can he be? It almost breaks her. Almost, but not quite.

There is a long pause as he returns to the lawn mower. She composes herself.

"Andrew, please stand up for a minute. Please." Pleading replaced by building anger.

He slowly stands. Wipes his hands on his pants.

She has her shoulders back, chest out, neck stretched, eyes wide, painted lips parted. Eyes so painfully eager to be seen.

He sees her "new" breasts for the first time, steps back and looks at her again, leans in, looking into her eyes.

I'm holding my breath.

"Kiko, what the fuck... you, what happened to you? I, I... mean... You grew up! You, look so fine. You do."

Jesus, he finally starting to see how she has changed. I hope he really, really looks at her. He's needs to get past her looks... she is a lot more... well. He sees what he wants to see, what she wants him to see. Good for you, Kiko. Good for you.

They go to the movies. I hope she fucks his brains out. She deserves it. She earned it.

It's almost noon. I sit on my front porch with a drink in my hand. My bottle of Gilbert's on the end table, smoking my Kent's, drinking my gin. In seven days, I'll be a free woman. I'll have my life back.

Look at me. I've already started celebrating. I pour myself another drink. I will count the hours to my liberation. I surely will.

Dead End

She wakes beside me in our shabby motel room and gives me a half interested who are you, where are we, look. It passes quick. It don't really matter. What matters to her is, where is the bathroom?

I point. She goes in. She out in three minutes.

In the light of day, I see her. Junky thin, pale, homely face. Pretty deserted her long ago along with hope and happiness.

Her habit's coming down, she's starting to shake and fade.

"Hey, hey I had a nice time. Awww, man could you help a sister out... just anything... a dollar or two... anything…"

I have a twenty, a five, and a bus ticket to get me from El Paso back to Oakland. I give her the five.

A little light in her eyes now.

I show her the twenty-year-old picture again, an eight-year-old Brown-skinned boy with his six-year-old light skinned sister, happy together.

She barely pretends to look. She shakes her head, no. She's squeezing Lincoln to death.

I take my wallet into the bathroom with me.

I don't see her stop halfway to the door, spin on her six-inch heels, cross to the picture, stare hard, and look sick.

I don't see her bite right through her lower lip. I don't see the flood of tears or hear the choked back scream.

I miss it all taking a piss.

Just another dead end.

Black and Blue

Man, in my community color still rules; white you all right, brown stick around, black get back. And sometimes we be so black we be blue. And the rules flip on you sometimes. Sometimes they do a back flip when you blue-black.

My papa has a blue-black cousin, Bob White. Our Bob White don't sing or fly. We call him Mr. Blue. We kids call him Uncle Blue.

He special and he know it, like some kind of royalty out of our African past. Black people gave him an extra measure of respect. We kids just get the hell out of his way. Uncle Blue do not play at all, a serious man with a serious walk and no talk. Rarely talked. Quiet and serious. But when he talks, we all listen: kids, adults and even the old folks. We shut the hell up and listen.

We going into Sumter with Uncle Blue and his oldest boy, Baby Blue. We take the wagon with the two gray mules, Cain and Abel. Go to the dry goods store. Go to the feed lot.

Walking to the dry goods store, a big white man in an apron talking to an older white woman, blocking our path. Did we go around them? Did Uncle Blue tip his hat, say good day and move on? No! Not at all. Uncle Blue stop. He wait impatient, for the white folks to get the hell out of his way. You don't do that shit in Sumter South Carolina in 1956. Not unless you got a death wish.

The white woman see him first. All of the color drain out of her. Her hand go to her throat. She step back.

Big apron man turn to Uncle Blue.

"Nig... nig..." He trying to say: "Nigger what the hell is wrong with you?" He can't get it out. He stagger back toward his shop. Backs into his shop.

"Sor... sorr..." He trying to say: "I'm sorry." But, he can't get that out either.

That little old white woman follow us to the feed lot. She respectful about it. She stay well back.

By the time we get the wagon loaded, there are three or four white folks watching us at a respectful distance. The sheriff come and join them. He not in no uniform or wearing no badge. He stand with them others.

What the hell these white folks want? They not a lynch mob. They acting like they in church. No, they acting like they seeing a prophet or something out the Bible. But what do they want?

Loaded. Baby Blue and I up on the seat. Uncle Blue walk back to that old white woman that was following us. Stop in front of her. He poke her in the chest with his finger.

"You healed." He says that.

The noise, the sound that come out of her, is everything in her, all the pain and joy and despair and hope and suffering. Painful to hear that sound. Fell to her knees sobbing, rejoicing.

We drive away.

Later, I ask Baby Blue what that was all about. "A show, white folks expect a show." That's what Baby Blue tells me.

Homeward Bound

I do it on a cold December day in Oakland, California. I sign the papers. Pass the physical. In three days, I will belong to the United States Air Force, freedom for me, freedom from her.

I get off the Army bus from the Induction Center at the Greyhound Bus Station in Oakland, stepping light and easy and right on time.

"The bus to Sacramento is now loading on track three. All ticketed passengers should proceed to track three."

I think I can start to breathe again, be my own self again. Hard to remember the last time I was free… six years is a long-time… I would rather not go back to her house, rather not even see her again. Only I need to put a period to this six-year sentence, get some answers at least.

If I close my eyes, I can remember free - the humid, heavy scented air of South Carolina. I can smell freedom. I can feel freedom in the soles of my feet.

I break up the dirt clods with my bare feet. I pick up and marvel at the size of some of the earth worms. Grandpa and I have on our bib overalls and our old stained straw hats. I'm eight years old. I was up at five, and had breakfast with my grandparents.

This is where I belong.

I help harness Sampson, our mighty mule. I lead him out to the plow. I hitch him up.

We don't have a tractor, just Sampson and Bessie, our plow horse. Back in 1938 Grandpa got burned bad in a tractor accident. He almost died. They did skin grafts all across his back. No more tractors after that.

Grandpa said that was the worst time of his life. The pain was so bad he wished he was dead. He told me that sometimes you don't know good luck from bad.

I think he was just lucky to be alive.

"Grandpa, why can't colored people use the library in Sumter?"

He nods his head to acknowledge my question. He will take his time in answering, maybe days. He takes my questions seriously. I appreciate that.

The rain comes. Big fat drops, warm and soothing, a spring shower.

Sampson stops. He looks back at us. Sampson will not plow in the rain.

Grandpa said Sampson will not work himself to death. He will not plow in a wet field. He knows what load he can pull, and what load he can't. A horse will die in the harness trying. Sampson won't.

You can beat Sampson. You can beat him to death in the harness, but he won't work himself to death and do that job for you.

And look out if you beat Sampson, be careful now, because he'll use his stone grinding teeth on you. He'll kick you over the barn and straight into the grave. He won't have no mercy, none at all.

"This is Berkeley. This is our first stop, Berkeley. Our next stop will be Richmond."

No mercy at all. I remember that now. I remember when I'm eleven and Grandpa is dying, cancer, no mercy there.

The house is full: my three uncles and three aunts and their families, my mother, a hundred cousins and relatives I don't know, and don't want to know.

They're in our house, disrupting things, and bringing noise, and motion, and something else I can't put my finger on, but don't like.

I ignore them.

I do the chores.

My cousin Emma arrives from her boarding school. She is six months older than me. She hugs me and joins in doing the chores. There is nothing to say.

Emma and I do everything we can think of to stay out of the house. At last, we sit on the porch and pretend to play checkers. We wait.

Uncle Ed comes for us. He leads us to the dark bedroom. Emma grabs my hand. We go in holding hands.

I'm not crying. I'm not. Not a tear.

We split up and go to opposite sides of the bed. We each take up one of his big rough hands. We hold them tight.

Uncle Ed slips out, closing the door quietly.

Grandpa pulls us close. Looks at us with weak, watery eyes, glazed over eyes. I know he sees us clearly. He sees through us. He knows all our tricks and games and fears.

He pulls us even closer. He speaks in a low voice, as rough as his hands. We can barely hear. His breath is hot and sickly. "Take care of each other… and Grandma… be… be your own self… be… kind…"

And it is over. We flee out the house. We run. We run like its summer time, and we are chasing the good life, chasing life itself. We run until we drop.

"This is Richmond. Richmond passengers debark here. Our next stop is Vallejo. Vallejo is our next stop."

My country life stops and detours, when grandma dies six months later.

My mother comes for me.

I once asked my Grandpa what my mother was like when she was little. He answered me two days later: "Sharp, quick, tough, tough as old leather. She picked up things real quick. She made her own path."

Now, Miss-Sharp-and-Quick is back here to pick me up, to try to sell the farm, to take me away. Talking like she owns stuff here. Talking like she owns me.

I hate her.

Uncle Ed and Uncle Ross and Miss-Follows-Her-Own-Path are taking it all apart. I get sick of it. I confront them. They can't sell Sampson. That's it. Period. No discussion. He deserves retirement. He's worked hard. No glue factory for him.

Uncle Ross tries to explain why it is impossible to keep the mule, the cost and all the work. Miss-Sharp-and-Quick chimes in. I ignore them. I turn to Uncle Ed. I offer my inheritance from my grandparents if he'll take me and Sampson. I promise to take care of Sampson.

We take a walk. We strike a deal on Sampson. Uncle Ed will keep Sampson for five dollars a month for feed. I can work that off when I come home in the summers. He says he can't take me without my mother's approval. We shake hands.

I talk to Miss-Sharp-and-Quick. She ain't either, more like Dull-and-Slow. I offer her my inheritance if she lets me stay with Uncle Ed. I tell her that she don't need me. She hasn't needed me for twelve years. I have nearly ten thousand dollars. I offer it all to her.

She turns to ice, and then to steel. We stand there toe to toe. She says I'm spoiled rotten. I need a firm hand. There are more opportunities in California than I could ever imagine. She has already moved to accommodate me.

We are on the train the next morning.

I'm not leaving her. I'm escaping her. We are almost in Vallejo. That was quick. I wish I could have turned eighteen that quick.

"We are now arriving at Vallejo. This is Vallejo."

I remember my arrival in Sacramento six years ago.

We arrive at 3:00 am in a Yellow cab. My first cab ride following my first train ride. I'm not impressed with either.

The trip has not been an easy one on either of us. I was civil, polite, obedient, distant, and very angry.

She is anxious, uneasy, and short tempered, always on the edge of striking out. She tries, but she's not used to having to meet my needs. She's a lone wolf. She did try, but I am indifferent to her effort.

It's a small house with three bedrooms and one bathroom. The way she opens the door, the way she looks around, the care with which she has furnished it, all say it's her prized possession, her safe harbor.

She's so glad to be home that for a moment she forgets I'm even there.

Fine with me because it's a tiny little box with no basement or upstairs or attic rooms. And the yards are too small to even have a decent garden. Worst of all, there are other little boxy homes so close you can hear your neighbors fart.

I really don't understand what she is so proud of.

I have not been a good son, or even a good roommate. I let my anger, and fear poison me, and her. I turned her place of refuge into a place she dreaded coming home to.

"Our next stop is Davis. We may be arriving behind schedule. There appears to be an accident ahead of us."

I pay my way. I do the yard work. I get up early and fix our breakfast. I wash up the dishes and keep the house clean and neat. I pick up after her. She hates it.

The second week there, I'm picking up her shoes from the kitchen. She snaps. "Hey, put my fucking shoes down! You don't touch my things! You, moping around here like you the only one to ever lose someone. You have been a perfect little shit! I wish the fuck I had left you with your uncle Ed."

I jump about two feet in the air and drop the shoes like they're on fire. In my whole life, no grown up has ever cursed at me or screamed at me like that. Grandpa never raised his voice to me or Emma. I never heard him utter a curse word.

She is amazed at my response, "Andrew! What the fuck is the matter with you? I didn't even hit you."

I'm at a loss at how to respond. I walk out the door and down the street, to the park. I'm not sure how to handle the screaming and the yelling. It hurts worse than a whipping. After a while, I return to the house. She's there smoking and looking angry. She gives me some kind of half-ass apology. I ignore her. I start toward my room. I turn back. I walk up to her.

"I'm not a mule or a horse. If you hit me, I will hurt you."

Her face just freezes solid. Her eyes squeeze down to slits. The veins in her neck stand out like a road map. I can hear her teeth grinding. She hisses at me between clenched jaws. "You don't, you don't even know... you..." At least, that's what it sounds like she's saying. She jerks away from me. She's shaking and making a funny kind of growling noise, as she slams the front door. I go to bed. I don't know when she came back.

Next day, I tell her I don't want to be here, and she doesn't want me here, so send me home. We wrangle for a while, and we both agree to try to do better, and if things don't improve, we can look at me living with Uncle Ed at the end of the school year.

And things do get a little better for a while, until I dig up the backyard to put in a garden. A surprise for her. She heard me turning the soil on a sunny spring Saturday morning. She comes to see what I'm doing. She opens the back door. She turns bright red. Then she turns as pale as a ghost. She is speechless. She can't even curse me. She just eases back into the kitchen, and softly closes the back door. I go to check on her. I think she's dying or something. She's sitting on the kitchen floor with the phone receiver held to her ear. In her other hand is a bottle of red wine. She's drinking from the bottle. She don't look at me at all. "Go pack." That's all she says. I ask her if she's OK, and she gives me a look that would turn water to vinegar. I go pack. I sit on the fender of the old Ford Super DeLux with my hopes high and fingers crossed. I could already smell the sweet, heavy country air.

Misfortune, misunderstandings, and mistakes ruled our lives. Uncle Ed's injured in a farm accident. Aunt Ellen, Emma's mother, my next-best hope of escape, is in the midst of a nasty divorce. These two were our safety valves. Our emergency escape hatches. It makes us both a little crazy with anger and disappointment to lose both of these. We do not handle our disappointments well.

All that stuff is almost over now. Six years of our lives spent grinding each other up. Barbed-wire skin rubbed against sandpaper hide. We never clicked. We had better and worse, but it was never good for very long.

"We are arriving in Sacramento. This is our final stop. Please collect all your belongings. This is Sacramento. Thank you for riding Greyhound."

I'm a mile from her home. I walk there. I shower. I pack. I wait for her. She comes in with her briefcase, purse and a box of chicken. I look at her. I really look at her for the first time in a long time. She's exhausted, dead on her feet, running on fumes.

I don't know what to say or do. I helped make her like this. I never really tried. I wallowed in self-pity and fear. I ran on high-octane anger with a slow-burning engine. She's not a good mother. No patience. Don't like touching or being touched. She had me when she was only fourteen. My father, "a boy who promised her things." That's all she told me. She's stingy with my history. I'm generous with my resentment. It's just who she is, a loner. I can help her with that.

She knows something is going to happen. She feels the storm brewing. She puts the chicken and her other stuff on the floor. She kicks off her heels. She stands there facing me. A tall, wiry thirty-two years old, light skinned, black woman ready for one final winner take all grudge match with her only child.

"Why did you even come home every year? You were never happy there. You came in angry and left angrier, angry at me, at everyone. Why did you come back at all?"

She crosses her arms under her breasts. She looks at me all rigid and cold.

"Why did you even bring me out here in the first place? I have never been able to figure that out."

She takes a deep breath and looks away from me.

She gives me stiff words. "You got bus fare, Andrew? You got a place to stay tonight?" Her anger is barely suppressed.

"Answer me. I just want to know. Why did you hate us all so much?"

She turns and opens the front door.

"You stay safe Andrew." I can hear the anger bubbling up in her words.

I walk over and snatch the door from her. I slam the door shut. I lean against the door. I face her.

"I won't bother you again. I promise. Every year you came home for a week? You didn't want to be there. You were hateful to everyone. So why come every year? Why come at all?"

"Andrew, get the fuck out of my house. Go before it get ugly up in here." This is her real voice. The one I hear in my head all the time.

I shake my head, cross to the couch, pick up my travel bag.

"It been ugly since day one. Since I got here."

"Andrew, did your grandfather ever beat you? Hurt you?"

I cross to her. Quick. I'm up in her face. "Never, never even yelled at me like... like... He only spanked Emma and me once. Shit, Emma hit me a lot harder than he did that time. Why did you ask me that?"

"Back up, Andrew, back up off me now. He was.... Just back up off me."

I back off her. I don't know why the question disturbed me so much. I have overstayed my welcome by about six years.

She is standing strong as iron, sturdy as an oak. Her eyes are fixed on me. I can't figure out the look on her face, not anger, or frustration or impatience, something else entirely. It scares me, chills me to the bone. I move toward the door. She blocks me.

"Never took a belt to you? A razor strop? An ironing cord? His fist?"

I try to step around her. She steps in front of me.

"Ever slap you? Backhand you off your feet?

I'm sweating. I feel dizzy, a little dizzy.

"Why, why are you, asking?" I swallow hard.

She turns her back to me, unbuttons her blouse. She takes it off and drops it on the floor. She has on a little silk undershirt. She pulls it over her head. I close my eyes, squeeze them shut. I turn my head.

"Andrew. Andrew look. Look at me! Fucking look at me Andrew."

I turn toward her. I take a deep breath. I'm trembling, shaking like I got a bad fever. I look.

Her back, her back is a rugged landscape of scars, welts and craters. A tortured, twisted battlefield... her ruined back... her abused back... like old injured leather.

I reach out a trembling hand past my fears, through my anger. I reach and reach and reach, stretch my fingers, my hand touches, touches, touches her back... touches my mother's back.

We sit across from each other at the kitchen table. My hand burns from the touch of her back. I flex it open and close. It still burns.

Everything is upside down and broken. I feel like Humpty Dumpty. I don't believe her. Her backs not a lie. The scars are real. It doesn't prove he did it.

I squeeze out the critical questions of my life. "Why did you bring me out here with you? Why did you come back there every year?"

Her voice is raspy, harsh, intense. "Fuck you Andrew! Fuck you! You had every fucking thing: love, respect, fucking kindness... kindness... things I never had you... you had the best of them... I hated you for that and I hated him for giving it to you..."

Her voice trails off, but her eyes grow more intense hotter, angrier.

"After the tractor accident he changed ... changed in time to be a better parent to you than I could ever be. Jesus, even when he changed, he found a way to fuck with me, to keep hurting me. A better parent... him... me..."

She leans into me with those angry eyes and taunt face. At that moment, I'm not sure what's she going to do. She looks capable of anything.

I'm not going to fight her. I can't. I close my eyes. I wait for my mother's touch.

WAR
HERE ... AND THERE

The Platform

"Nigger, please, integration's a bad joke on poor colored folks. It's a mean, low down trick you talented tenth, college clowns pulling on your own people, people that don't know any better."

That's Houston ranting and raving on one of his favorite subjects. It's below freezing in Philly on this December night in 1962. But, Houston's running hot and not feeling the cold at all.

"You sound like a smarter than average Negro that has first-hand experience with that tricky old integration. How can a smart guy like you let integration play a bad joke on you?"

That's Walter, my home boy from California. I'm Teofilo Jackson, and we're on our way to the EL to the bus station and back to McGuire Air Force Base.

"Man, you don't need experience. You need common sense. How many white people did you see up in the projects tonight? They got all the colored people all over this country jammed into slums and all black neighborhoods. You think white people gonna move into those neighborhoods? Most black folks can't afford no place else. And, them that can ain't gonna be welcome in any white neighborhood north or south."

I love it when these two get going. They provide enough hot air to raise the temperature a few degrees, even on a night like this. We moving from the project area to a nicer part of town, meaning the white part of town, but we're still alert. Philly can turn mean real quick, no matter the color of the neighborhood.

"Houston, you live in integrated barracks, eat in an integrated chow hall and do the same work as the white boys do for the same pay. You sit wherever you want on the EL or the bus. Black people everywhere deserve the integration you got here man."

We come to the long flight of steel steps leading up to the EL platform. We pause and check out our surroundings. Our gloved hands grip the rails as we climb, these steps can ice up in this kind of weather. We hold the conversation until we check out the platform and see who's there.

There's no one there. We move to the back of the platform, out of the light. We had a run-in with some project thugs in North Philly. Now, we treat this town like a war zone.

I interject my two cents, "I see where you guys are coming from. You both sound, right and wrong to me. I couldn't live down south, but I don't see integration coming anytime soon to my neighborhood in Oakland."

There are voices coming from the bottom of the steps. We shut-up and listen-up, sounds like a man and woman, sounds white and too loud, drunk maybe.

Two blonde heads appear. She's laughing and holding on to him.

He has on a wool top coat, expensive looking, and black pants with a shiny black strip running up the leg, and dress shoes; they're about our age.

I know about coats now. My California jacket couldn't deal with this east coast cold. My first major purchase here was a good wool top coat.

She has on a fur coat and heels.

No hats. White people are like that. I pull my watch cap down over my ears. I get colder just watching them.

They don't even see us, or even think to check out the platform. This is their world. They're loud and drunk. They don't have to be careful, lucky them.

Houston sighs, shakes his head.

Walter steps out of the shadows.

"Hey, you guys all right?"

The both turn and look at Walter. They look him up and down like they found a turd on their dinner plate. They turn away giggling and hugging each other.

Walter steps back to us. They make us nervous with their noise and antics and standing out there in the light. Without any discussion, we all come to the same conclusion at the same time; we need to move to a different platform.

But it's too late. Three young brothers stomp up the steel steps smiling like miners who've struck gold.

One moves over to the woman's side, the other steps behind the blonde man. The leader addresses the white guy, "Man, you got the time?"

Striped pants can't ignore the thug standing there breathing down on him. He sighs in exasperation and shoots his cuff to check his watch.

The leader hits him with a powerful short right hand to the jaw. I hear a bone crack. One more sigh from striped pants as he hits the platform.

The woman's finally awake to what's happening. She starts to scream. The brother by her side grabs her by the throat, stifling her scream. He leans in and whispers loudly in her ear, "Take off your coat and your jewelry, and we won't hurt you. Be quick now."

She tries to turn her head to look at us. Her captor follows her gaze. He sees us.

"Hey," he alerts the other two who're stripping her date of his coat, gloves and other valuables.

They all turn toward us. We keep our hands in our pockets, like we might have something more useful and dangerous in our pockets than our hands. We don't.

The leader takes a step toward us. All three of us take a step toward him. He stops and signals his partners to hurry up.

He now has his hand in his coat pocket. He keeps his eyes locked on us. The other two keep glancing up at us as they pillage.

They have everything they want from the couple. We all wonder what's coming next.

The leader gives a hand sign to the mugger by the woman. The robber taps her on the back of the head. There is a soft thud. She plops to the ground.

The other two bandits turn toward us.

I'm not cold anymore. I stare at my counterpart a few feet away from me, about my age, size and color. He has the fur coat in one hand a sap in the other. Moms, remember me for the good things I did. I'm ready now for whatever happens.

The leader motions for the other two to go on. They move out quickly.

With his hand in his pocket, the leader backs to the steps. He turns away and flies down the steps.

We let out a collective sigh of relief.

"We should check on them."

I'm ignored. "We should-"

"We should run like hell to the next stop."

Walter has grabbed my arm as he's talking.

"Take the first train. Sit in separate cars." Houston's moving toward the steps as he replies.

Walter's pulling me in the same direction. "You right. They'll be looking for three niggers. Any three niggers will do."

We zoom down the steps, but we walk to the next stop. Running niggers are always a target and are nearly always found guilty of something, or shot dead for nothing.

I still see the couple sprawled on the cold concrete; coatless, gloveless, helpless, bleached skulls and pale hands in party clothes. It all feels so wrong. I know Walter and Houston was right, but it still feels wrong today over fifty years later.

War Stories

Coming up out of North Carolina in the 1930s was no easy passage. My folks were share croppers out in Union County. Sharecropping just another name for slavery. Only a few ways out of that trap, you could cut and run in the middle of the night, or get mad and talk back to some white man. That would get you out in a pine box. Or, you could drown in drink, or die in harness. Them was your ways out.

My papa beat the odds. He was a silver smith by trade, as was his men folks all the way back from Africa, but they wouldn't let him be that. Papa worked in the old, falling down barn at night in secret. His brother, Uncle Henry, brought him the silver and the orders. He did silverware, plates, bowls, candle holders, and even jewelry, for rich white folks in Durham and Charleston. He got cash for his works.

At settling up time, the plantation owner said,"Jonas, you got to do a little better, work a little harder, next year. You still fifty dollars in arears. Next year, if you work hard ... Hell, who knows? You might even make a little money."

My father had the Owner write down and initial the amount owed, so he could show my mother, to prove to her that they was still in debt. The owner played along. Mama and papa had already packed everything they owned on Uncle Henry's old Ford truck.

My papa counted out five ten-dollar bills to the owner. The owner turned bright red and almost choked on his cigar.

They was half way to Charlotte while the Owner was still choking on that cigar.

That's how I got to be born in Charlotte instead of a sharecropper's cabin.

When I was seventeen I joined the Army just to get out of the South.

I just traded my South, for South Korea. I was an infantry man in the Eighth Army under General Ridgeway. Got captured up around Pusan, me and a young GI Chinaman. We thought we was dead for sure.

There was this North Korean officer we called Flat Face. Mean as a junk yard dog. He was the interrogator. Some of us came back from interrogation in some sad shape. Them boys walked in, but they had to be carried out.

Others never came back at all.

When my turn came I pissed on myself when they came for me. Flat Face just sat me down and talked about jazz, wanted to know about Miles and Stan Kenton, wanted to talk about Oscar Peterson. That was all. He sent me back in the same shape I came in.

That night about midnight he came and got me and the Chinaman and walked us out of camp. We knew he was going to kill us. We was both praying as hard as we could. It was so damn cold that I was afraid I would freeze to death before he shot us. We must have walked miles in that frozen night.

He stopped us. He told us our lines was about four hundred yards over the low hill directly in front of us.

We froze. We didn't know what to do. We didn't understand what was going on. He kicked us each in the ass and boy; we flew over that hill.

I never understood why he let us go. I think about it a lot lately. I wonder what happened to Flat Face. I hope he made it through the War. I hope he got to listen to some good jazz.

A Tale of Two Sergeants

I just got fired. I didn't see it coming at all. Shit, it took us all by surprise; the whole Tracking Unit and the Air Surveillance Officer or ASO too. Sergeant Ricks' first official day on the job and he fires my black ass. Replaces me with Airman Second Class Burton Beck; a lazy ass, screw up white boy from Western Ohio. Shit!

And the bad thing about being fired is I can't even complain about it. Sergeant Ricks is doing it by the book. Beck is the senior airman on our crew. He should be the lead. Me, I'm the lowest ranking man on the crew. I should never have been the lead.

Ricks is from South or North Carolina; I think, but I don't think this is about race. I think Ricks is a by the books' kinda guy. Just my luck.

I try to talk to Sergeant Ricks at the end of shift.

"Sarge, I understand why you made the change, but you should look at Korn or Flicks for lead. Beck... Beck is a fuck up."

Ricks is sharp as a tack. Creases in his tailored uniform like razors. Shoes like black glass. A perfect crew cut, flat as a table.

He is serious Air Force. His voice is clipped and slurred, in a rhythm based on his attempts to weed the south out of his voice and give it an east coast sound. The south sneaks back in and sabotages him again and again.

"Airman, this ain't personal. Sergeant Kirkland strongly suggested that I keep you on as lead. I can't do that. Fuck up or not, Beck carries the rank. He has to carry the weight as lead."

And that is that. Ricks brushes past me to talk to the ASO.

So, I think the shit can't be more disappointing until I talk to Chicago. Chicago is the only other Black on our crew. There are only four blacks in the whole Operations Section. He's my running buddy. I look to him for a little support, or at least sympathy. He surprises the hell out of me.

He agrees with Ricks in removing me as lead. He thinks Kirkland screwed things up when he made me lead over other senior airmen. "Teofilo, man, you act like you know it all, like you got some right to be the boss. That's bullshit man. Your shit stinks just like everybody else."

"Chicago, I been lead for over six months. Why didn't you say something before now? What's with you man?"

"Hey, what's there to say? Kirkland and the ASO both thought you was their big, bright, house nigger. You made the rest of us look bad so you could look good."

I'm stunned, shocked speechless.

Chicago and I were in tech school together. We came to McGuire at the same time. We been all over Jersey, Philly, The City, AC and DC with Chicago. We been in some real tight spots. Shit, the nigger sound like he hates my guts. What the hell's up with that? Look, I didn't lose any money or privileges when I got fired. Shit, being lead was a lot of extra work for no extra pay.

We're part of the Air-Defense Command. Our job is to detect, identify, and destroy enemy aircraft attacking the U.S. That's truly an unlikely scenario, but that's our mission. We are an aircraft radar tracking unit. We work on sixteen big metal desk consoles, with big-ass CRT screens, like black-and-white TVs. There's a small digital information display a telephone connection, and a headset on each console. We work with this four-story computer, inside a block house, with walls three feet thick. The computer takes the feed from radar stations in our sector, merges it, and displays it on our screens.

The screens display aircraft in the air in the New York City - New Jersey area.

We track, or associate, raw radar data with computer generated symbols. Sometimes it can be very intense, exacting work. Most of the time we struggle to keep awake. It's about as exciting as watching paint dry. We work in a "blue room," where the temperature is a constant sixty-four degrees. There is easy-on-the-eyes blue lighting, to make it easier to work our radar displays.

Our tracking unit, full crew of eight or nine, splits in half to work three swing and three midnight shifts. The crew comes back together to work three-day shifts. We then have three or four days off. The changing shifts take some getting used to. On our shifts, we work an hour on and an hour off, with half the crew working while the other half is in the break room. We generally only work four hours of every eight-hour shift. We don't complain about that part of our jobs. The lead is in charge of half the crew on every shift. The crew chief, a staff or tech Sergeant, leads the other half.

Hell, no one really wants to be lead. You have to show up earlier than the rest of the crew; get briefed by the crew chief you are relieving; review logs and read reports, and check out the telephones and each CRT. And you take shit from the ASO and the Weapons Section officers, our interceptor controllers.

We have a squadron of F-106s that intercept unknown aircraft. This kind of intercept is extremely rare.

Mostly, we run training intercepts on our own fighters pretending to be unknowns.

Losing my lead job hurts. Shit, I was good at it. But, this shit with Chicago; man that is unreal. We depend on each other out in the world and on the base. I need to figure that mess out quick. Brother man is tripping. I need to find out why.

And to make my day a complete disappointing disaster, when I finally get off work and call my girl, Joy, she's out on a date.

I go talk to Edward, my best buddy and my fellow Californian. His advice: stay on the good side of Sergeant Ricks. Help where I can, but don't get in his way.

Just then that fool comes on the radio singing If You Wanna Be Happy. I turn that shit off quick. Royce, the brother who handles FAA coordination in our unit, knocks and enters before we can respond. He comes in with a cold six-pack of Schlitz. Chicago has told him about my demotion; told him with enthusiasm and satisfaction.

"Niggers will be niggers. The funny thing is none of the white boys complained about you being lead."

I correct Royce. "Beck complained-"

"Nigger please, Beck don't count. Nobody listens to his bullshit. Mark my word, the white boy's in your corner. The ASO is in your corner. You just got to keep an eye on Chicago."

After chow, I try to talk to Chicago. I ask how I make the crew look bad, so I could look good.

He says I read the tech manuals and systems updates on my breaks at work, and that I talk to the tech reps who help us run the system. He believes I do this to show everyone else up. I believe the boy done gone stone crazy.

When I first came to Operations, and I sit down at my 144 square inch CRT, and saw the constant flow of aircraft coming and going out of New York and New Jersey, and aircraft hundreds of miles out over the Atlantic, I thought this is how God must see the world looking down on everything. It was an awe-inspiring view.

I wanted to learn everything I could about the computer and the radar systems. I did it to satisfy my own curiosity, not to put anyone else down.

Chicago goes on to note that I'm the only one of the six from our tech school class, not to be promoted to Airman Second Class. He claims that my know-it-all attitude is probably why I haven't been promoted. I look at him real hard. He just stares back at me. I wonder what is going on in that thick head of his. Does he really believe what he's saying, or is this just some bullshit he created to justify his dislike of me? Was he ever my friend?

I leave shaking my head.

He's right about the promotion. The promotion to Airman Second Class is almost automatic. And I know for a fact that my promotional evaluations were superior to every one of my classmates. I know this because Sergeant Sandoval, our Operations Exec, told me so, and because Ham, our Ops Clerk, confirmed it. Ham even violated all kinds of regulations, showing me the evaluations.

Sandoval, the ASO, and even Major Ferris, the Chief of Operations, have gone to bat for me, all to no avail. Well, I sure as hell must have pissed off someone other than Chicago.

I go from work to the gym, workout on the free weights for an hour. I swim ten laps in the pool to cool down.

The next morning I still don't understand why I haven't been promoted. I'm still demoted. And to the best of my knowledge Chicago still hates me.

On the bright side, my life does have continuity. More continuity than I realize. The shit starts as soon as I get to work. I'm ten minutes early out of force of habit. As the lead, I was required to be ten minutes early. Ricks is talking to the oncoming and the departing ASOs. Sergeant Wood, the crew chief about to be relived, wants to join the conversation. He motions for me to take his station. Ricks stops his conversation to tell Wood that I'm no longer lead.

Sergeant Wood, not known for his tact or subtlety, responds. "So, where the fuck is your fucking lead?"

The ASOs and everyone else turn to look at Ricks.

Ricks turns to look at me. "You're not due up here for another five minutes. Why don't you come back in five." I can tell by his words and his attitude, he blames me for this bad start to his second day on the job. I start to leave and the departing ASO makes the situation a hundred times worse when he asks me if the reinitiating range has changed since our last mission.

Ricks' steps in with the correct answer. "The range for reinitiating is bumped up from fifty to one-hundred miles."

The ASOs and Wood all turn to me for conformation. They consider me the resident expert on this shit. They all realize their mistake at the same time, but it is too late. Ricks is a bright red, and we can all hear him gritting his teeth.

I make a hasty departure.

I bump into Beck at the elevator. He makes some smart remark. I ignore him. He takes offense. He orders me to go back into the Air Surveillance blue room with him.

That is how my day started.

It goes downhill from there.

We run a mission. We have one of our interceptors designated as an unknown aircraft, and our controllers over in Weapons run intercepts on the "unknown." It is easy money stuff. We run these all the time. But Ricks' has new rules and procedures. They confuse not only the controllers, but the men in his own unit. The intercept is fucked up.

Ricks is on our cases immediately.

The ASO is all over Ricks.

The pilots are pissed at the controllers.

And the controllers are pissed at the ASO.

At the end of a very long day, Ricks takes me aside and reads me the riot act. His voice is all south now. I don't even try to defend myself. I just let his rage burn out. The bottom line – if I ever embarrass him again like that, he will have my one lonely little stripe, and I will be a cook or an Air Police on the most remote Air Force location in the world.

I drag myself out of the block house in a real poor state of mind.

But there is good news at the barracks. Joy has left me a message to have dinner with her family. I love Joy to pieces, but she can't cook a lick, which is fine because her father, Senior Master Sergeant Green, cooks like the Army chef he once was. And her brother, Honor, who we call Honey, is a grill master. I always eat good and plenty there.

Except this night. Joy has heard about my demotion. She wants to do something special for me. She cooks. Her father, her brother and I, we all try. We try hard, but the mashed potatoes are lumpy and runny and too salty. The steaks are too tough for our knives. Honor finds a caterpillar in his green salad. We move food around on our plates and try and distract Joy with our conversation. The meal ends badly when Honey "accidentally" knocks his plate onto the floor and in his rush to help his son, Sergeant Green sends his plate flying to the floor also.

Joy looks at me with fire in her eyes. "Teofilo Timothy Jackson, if you do, we are finished forever." I hesitate. I gather my courage. I take a bite of slimy rubbery green beans. I bolt for the bathroom. It ends with Joy in her room in tears, and the rest of us with queasy stomachs. Before she takes to her room, she promises me she will never try to do anything nice for me ever again.

I hope she just means cooking.

We men folk clean up and throw away the rest of the sorry excuse for a meal. I walk home hungry and beat. Of course, I missed dinner at the chow hall.

Well, tomorrow is a new day. A better day. It has to be.

But it ain't.

Sergeant Ricks threatens to put us all on report for our poor performance yesterday. He reads us his list of our sins and omissions from yesterday. According to him, we all need to be retrained. We try to explain what we thought went wrong, and how we can correct it. He say's we're on the brink of insubordination. We grumble ourselves back to work.

Beck is quiet, subdued and nervous like he missed his coffee fix.

We have a simulated mission this morning. The computer generates fake aircraft, and the controllers run intercepts without a real aircraft leaving the ground.

Sergeant Kirkland and I usually let one of the other airmen on our crew run these for the experience. They are low pressure low anxiety events.

But not today.

Beck is put in charge of the mission, with Chicago and Leeks working for him. Leeks and Beck are in a mutual hate relationship. Chicago ain't real fond of either of them. The mission is scrubbed after five minutes. Chicago has a bad phone or headset, and gets only half of the instructions from Beck. Leeks' CRT will not work correctly. The display blinks, and dies five minutes into the mission. Beck forgot to have the crew run equipment checks at the start of the shift.

The day doesn't get any better, but it doesn't get any worse, and for that we're all thankful.

I don't want to talk about our last day shift. All I can say is, if you took the first two-day shifts and multiplied them by a badness factor of ten, you would have our last day shift. I will say it ended with Ricks accusing the tracking unit of conspiring to get him fired. He tells us that he would see us all in hell before he would let that happen.

Well, at least I have three days away from the workplace shit. And this ain't Birmingham, where they rioting and blowing up black folks. I got to keep some perspective.

I'm wrong again, at least, about escaping the workplace bullshit. The word is, that Ricks is seeking an Article Fifteen, a disciplinary action, against Beck. He's accusing Beck of gross incompetence.

I go knock on Becks' door in the barracks. He opens the door. He sees me and starts to close the door. I push my way in.

Beck looks sick. He smells like three week-old dirty laundry and acidic, rotten fear. He drops into a chair at his table, and downs a quarter glass of vodka. He pours another drink. Eventually, he shows me a draft of the charges against him. There are thirteen. The accusation makes it seem as if Beck is the cause of every bad thing to happen since Cain slew Abel.

Enough is enough. Beck is a fuck up, but he's not the main cause of the problems in our Unit. I spend my time off organizing our Unit to list our grievances and concerns, and to meet with the ASO before we go back to work. I get everyone on board except Chicago.

I leave a message for Sergeant Ricks. He calls me right back. He gives us permission to speak to the ASO. "All of you huh? Go for it." He hangs up.

I get an appointment with the ASO at seven AM the day of our first shift. We meet in our debriefing room. There is a surprise for us in the form of a black Staff Sergeant, Sergeant Pear. He's our new Tracking Team Supervisor, our new crew chief.

Pear is older than dirt. He looks past retirement age. And he has no experience with our computer radar system. His whole history is in manual radar. Brother faces a huge learning curve. Plus, he's only a Staff Sergeant. He should at least be a Tech Sergeant this close to retirement. Shit, he may be a bigger fuck up than Beck. It looks like we have jumped from the frying pan into the fire.

I wish that Chicago was here. We need to figure out how to save Sergeant Pear from the same fate that Sergeant Ricks has just met.

The ASO asks us to hold off on our issues. He guarantees us things will be better.

We are agreeable, except for the Article Fifteen. I want that addressed right now. The ASO assures us there are no Article Fifteens pending against any airman in our Unit.

Sergeant Pear asks to speak to us alone.

Pear has each of us introduce ourselves, and talk about any problems we have in the tracking unit. He is low key with a southern drawl. Sounds like he might be from Carolina too. He, finally, hits us with his summary of our position.

"Fellas, I got less than three months left in this man's service. I just got back from Goose Bay. I should be processing out right now. I sure didn't choose this assignment, and you sure didn't choose me. We gonna make it work anyway. We gonna show em all. First, the ASO says you fellas know your stuff. So, you do your work like you know how. I won't get in your way. You keep me straight. I'll look out for you and get you fellas what you need to do your job. Is that a deal?"

It is a deal. We all shake hands on it.

Pear pauses for a moment and looks at each of us. "Last thing fellas is lead. Is there a problem there?"

The room goes quiet. Nobody says shit.

Beck finally speaks up. "We... we work good... better with aaah, aah, Teofilo, with Jackson as lead. We do."

Sergeant says he can't jump me over everyone else unless everyone agrees to it.

No problem there. Everyone agrees to me being lead. We all shake hands with Sergeant Pear on it. Everyone leaves but me. I ask to meet with Pear and the ASO. When the three of us are together, I bring up the issue of Chicago. I explain that he may not want to work for me. I want to find him a good position in our shop, but not on the tracking team.

Turns out the ASO, an Alabama white boy, thinks Chicago is wasted in tracking. He thinks Chicago can be a Radar Inputs Monitor Officer or RICMO. It is a prestige job. I agree that Chicago can master the job, and that it would be a "promotion" for him.

Back at work. We are under new management. The first day is a little rocky, but by the third day, we are back to normal. Thank God.

We run five live intercepts on day three. There are problems, but not because we fucked up.

I go to the debriefing with Sergeant Pear.

The controllers are still living in the Ricks' era, and are instantly on the attack against the Tracking Unit. My great fear is that Pear will be a handkerchief headed, Uncle Tom and cave into the officers.

No such thing. He's polite, diplomatic, but firm. He sticks to his guns. We, the Tracking Team, have prepared him for this debriefing. He's a quick learner. He has impressed everyone with his knowledge and his low-key country approach. There is only one sticking point. We lost track of a low level, below 1,000 feet, target aircraft. Lieutenant Wright, one of the controllers that we on the Tracking Team refer to as Lieutenant Dead Wrong, pushes the issue even after Pear shows that we lost our Cape May radar just before the intercept. Wright claims we should have opened up the adjacent radar sites to provide coverage.

Sergeant Pear explains that the RICMO tried that. Pear is being diplomatic in pointing out that the RICMO controls radar site coverage, not tracking. I'm less diplomatic. I get the floor and ask Wright if he has looked at the Radar Configuration Reports. Wright has no idea what I'm talking about. This is an obscure report that points out holes in our radar coverage. I suggest the Lieutenant reference that report and reconsider his complaint.

A very flustered Wright sits.

Major Ferris explains what the report is, and where it can be found.

Wright is devastated.

I'm delighted.

After the debriefing, Pear pulls my coat. He explains that Wright will spend the rest of his time here trying to get back at me. I now have an enemy where I could have had an ally, and that we all need allies. He disguises an order as a suggestion that I go make nice with Wright.

I eat crow. I go apologize to Wright in front of his crew, and Major Ferris.

Wright and I go for coffee.

I'm starting to see what might have disturbed Chicago about me.

I need to do a little soul searching.

Pear is with us for only thirty-five days. Thirty-five good, efficient, low key, uneventful days. We all miss him.

We get Ricks back.

A new changed, improved Ricks. Ricks Version 2.0. He and I have both learned a lot from Sergeant Pear.

Oh, I keep my job as lead.

When I look at Ricks and Pear, I find that I may be more than a little arrogant like Ricks. Shit, I want to be like Sergeant Pear.

It hurts to think I could be a Ricks. I want to have Pear's people skills, and wisdom, along with my technical skills. I guess I want everything. But, I won't get everything. I still don't know why I can't get promoted.

    But right now, I got to step. I got dinner at Joy's and thank God, she ain't cooking.

Firefight

Inspired by events recorded in Bloods: Black Veterans of the Vietnam War: An Oral History, by Terry Wallace

Ain't this some shit? We sitting out here in broad daylight doing a joint sweep with "B" Company, "B" Company, the greatest collection of fuckups to ever put on uniforms. Shit.

I'm on the 50-caliber machine gun on the halftrack, looking out over rice fields and huts. Any insurgents are long gone.

I fucked the Green Witch last night, smoked myself blind, so I'm cool with it. I can live with it. I close my eyes and I see the sweet, young country girl in the black pajamas, walking bare foot down a dirt road with a straw hat and a basket, walking to market. I pass her and smile. She looks away and turns back as I pass and gives me the sweetest smile. I-

Jo Jo is pulling on my pants leg and pointing toward a rice paddy at three o'clock. Fucking "B" Company has prisoners, three old men and a teenage girl or boy. Sergeant Rider and his new Platoon CO, Lieutenant Patton, and two other knuckle heads are herding the prisoners to the middle of the paddy. Rider forces his prisoners to kneel.

Fuck this shit! We ain't killing no old ass, brown people today. "Jo Jo, fire a warning over their heads."

There is the klack, klack sound of two M16 shots echoing over the rice paddy. The "B" Company fools drop like they been shot. The new CO falls into the shit with his men. Rider doesn't duck. He recognizes the tinny sound of our pop guns.

Rider looks directly at me. I wag my finger at him, no, no. I motion for him to let his prisoners go.

He gives me the finger. He raises his rifle to the back of one of the old men's head.

I click the safety off the 50. I see my squad members clicking off their safeties all around me, as "A" company gets ready to rock and roll in the morning mist, the fucking OK Corral in the wild, wild east.

Buck, our big, dumb ass, white, West Virginia sniper, targets Rider. Rider sees him line him up. I could kiss Buck.

Nobody in "B" Company has clicked off their safeties. The cowardly motherfuckers. I should light em up on GP. That's not me, that's the Green Witch talking, but that bitch is convincing.

Russell, with his AK-47 at the ready, wades over to the group in the rice field. He stops and shakes his head at Rider. Russell bends down and helps the old people up. He sends them all on their way.

The whole thing took about two minutes.

Our new platoon CO finally, at last, just begins to understand what happened. He is incredulous.

He demands we put our weapons down and prepare to face a court martial. The "B" Company Lieutenant arrives smelling like shit and demanding my arrest. I think the fool wants to pull his sidearm. Rider hangs back looking for an opportunity to do dirt. Ain't none of us giving up shit. We decide this shit ends here and now in the field.

"B" company is now getting all loud and angry, like they going to do something, but that time has passed.

First Sergeant Garcia to the rescue. He has been watching the whole show and ain't said shit. Garcia runs "A" Company no matter who the Captain is, and God help any Lieutenant that gets in his way. Garcia only about five-six, but don't nobody fuck with him.

He takes the new COs and Rider down the road apiece. The Lieutenants are jumping around mad as hornets.

Garcia talks sense to them. They brand new and on their first day in the field, they lose control of their companies. Our Lieutenant, Turner, was so slow to act that he might be the one facing court martial. That shuts Turner up.

And Patton was executing prisoners in violation of our Standing Operating Orders. Garcia states the SOO letter perfect.

That shuts up Patton. Patton so new that he don't know that no one follows the SOOs. The resolution is that Garcia will figure out a punishment for me, as the ring leader, and that Rider will go over the SOOs with Patton.

Now, "B" Company hates me worse than they hate the gooks. Fuck em all. Next time, I will light em up.

Garcia has harsh words for me. "Corporal Wilson, don't you ever pull that fucking shit again unless you got all the bars and stars in the field of fire. If you leave one brass wearing motherfucker alive, we all fucked." My punishment, I do base guard duty rather than patrols, for one week.

We fuck the Green Witch and get ready for the next day. Shit, every day is a good day when you fucking the Witch and in Uncle Sam's Army. It's all good all the time.

Court Martial of Samuel James Wilson

"All right, Captain Clay, it's your turn to drink from the bitter cup. You need to weave your peculiar brand of Southern gothic magic and turn this acerbic cup into a wine that'll astonish the palate and amaze the mind. You do understand me?"

I'm standing at attention. I'm the only JAG in the Office that's required to stand at attention like this. This Yankee colonel has a distinct bias against everything southern.

"Sir-"

The uncouth three-hundred-pound polar bear in an Army uniform belches.

"You have the unparalleled good fortune to represent our most infamous client, Corporal Samuel James Wilson. This is a career maker son - or a heart breaker. Your simple task is to save that young soldier from the noose. You understand that, Tulane?"

The Yankee's a graduate of the Yale Law School. How he must despise even the very sight of my lily white, southern ass.

I'm at attention. I take a deep breath. "Colonel, Sir, if this solider did desert his unit as charged, if he did provide critical intelligence to the enemy that resulted in the devastating defeat at Camp Oswald, and if he was the consort of General Pham it may be beyond my power to-"

The Colonel comes out of his chair like some great white ICBM launched to bring death and destruction down on me and mine. It's a frightening sight to behold.

"Do you understand your orders Captain?"

"Sir, I-"

"Captain, do you understand your orders?"

"Yes Sir. I understand my orders, Sir."

He clenches and unclenches his paws. He looks at me as if I were a new, odd breed of imbecile. He shakes his head in disgust and points to the case files on his desk. I step forward and pick up the files. I stand at attention.

"Do not fuck this up Southern Comfort. A man's life's at stake here. In the eyes of your southern God of wrath, Wilson's worth more than the both of us combined. Understand that."

I don't understand that at all. Where did that observation come from? What does it mean?

I escape the Colonel's office with the disturbing idea that God has somehow found us wanting and favored a Negro deserter, coward and traitor, over me.

###

I work better from my quarters than in the office. I start with the pictures in the case file. I let them spill out of their envelopes and folders onto my kitchen table and the floor without order or direction. Some are covered by other pictures. Others are upside down. It doesn't matter. The important ones will reveal themselves. They always do.

The Negro corporal is not favored by God. He's going to hang. I know that. The Colonel knows that. God knows that.

I reach down and pick up a picture of a younger, pre-enlistment Wilson. He's standing beside a tiny, gray haired black woman. She's shooting an ice pick look at me, piercing my eyes, lacerating my heart, stabbing my soul.

    I fling the picture away, jump back away from the eyes. I'm shaking and short of breath. I leave the picture on the floor. I dash into my bedroom. My shaking hands remove the picture of me and my grandmother from the frame. I take care to avoid looking into her eyes. I return to the kitchen and use my picture to scoop up that other pictures from the floor. I put them both in a manila envelope and seal the envelope with my spit. I hide the envelope under my underwear in my dresser. Still shaken, I retreat to my big comfort chair; the brandy is warm and wonderful. After the second one, I return to the other pictures.

###

    I pick up a letter from an Army intelligence captain from the pile. It explains that there was no open case on Pham, but they have some pictures of her that were taken when investigating other bar girls as possible spies. The captain has circled Pham in these pictures.

    The picture I pick up is of four bar girls posing in a Negro bar. Two of the girls are ravishing. The third is big breasted with a pretty face, but not in the same league with the other two. I do not need the circle to recognize Pham. She's tiny, thin, shabbily dressed, poorly presented. She dominates the picture. The girls on either side of her leave ample distance between them and her out of respect. The two girls on Pham's right look in at her to understand how they should behave in this photo. Pham looks straight ahead, into me, sly, intelligent, in control. She's fearless. I do not try to stare her down. I handle the picture with great care.

Another brandy or two. How could Army Intelligence miss her? She has such presence in a picture! How the fuck could they miss her? A spy? Looking for a spy? Stupid fucks! There she was, the commander of the Home Defense Forces in Ha Binh Province, on display with all that power and authority, and they were looking for spies. I'm shaking with anger and frustration. She has the same kind of presence and power as the two women in my underwear drawer. How in the world could anyone miss that?

The knock on my door takes me by surprise. I check my watch. Its Seventeen-thirty hours. I have spent the whole day studying two pictures.

The Colonel has summoned me. He asks me how Wilson is holding up. I confess I've not yet visited Wilson.

His voice is kind. His tone is mild.

"Wilson has the whole weight of the United States Army crushing the life from him. He's in a hopeless, hapless position. He's a pariah. He's alone. He might just appreciate contact with the one person in the whole world who's obligated by law and morality to defend him."

The Colonel puts his heavy arm around my shoulder. At that moment, I fear for my life at the hands of this mad Colonel. I make it to the stockade in record time.

Wilson is dark chocolate brown with perfect white teeth and an athletic build. He's a handsome man. With a smile that lights up his whole face. I dislike him on sight. No, I disliked him on seeing his picture the first time. No, I disliked him from the first time I heard his name. It's not just that he's a Negro. I grew up in the company of Negroes. For the most part, I found them lazy and unreliable. There are exceptions to every rule that prove the rule. He may or may not be the exception. But, I dislike him in a more fundamental way that I find difficult to define.

He takes all this in at a glance. He understands I despise him. He has southern ways in his blood. We are kin. He still smiles at me and offers me his hand. I'm ashamed of myself. I can see, feel my grandmother turning her scorching gaze on me. It makes me hate him even more.

Introductions are over. We sit there in a comfortable silence. We know where we stand. I like it like this. No lies yet. I ask him to tell me his story.

She approached him in a bar. She insulted him. He teased her. Weeks later, he saved her from an attack by a Special Forces Sergeant. She was not grateful. He met her again in the company of some of his friends. They spoiled her transaction with a young GI and laughed at her.

He went back to "check on her." He touched her. They were wedded at that touch. They "fucked" over the next few months as often as they could until he realized who she was. They "fucked" one last time after that. They "fucked" while the three Northern Provinces were starting to fall and Camp Oswald was being decimated bad, bad timing. She arranged a car to take him back to an Army controlled area.

They never talked about military issues. She never asked. He never volunteered. They're not in love. It's much stronger than love. We leave it at that. I report back to the Colonel. It's nineteen-thirty. He's still in the office, waiting.

###

I believe him, every word. I know he's going to hang now. The other charges do not matter. He was having carnal knowledge of the author of the destruction of his comrades in arms while they were dying. He'll hang for that. All four charges against him are hanging charges. Even if I succeed in getting one or two dismissed or reduced, which is highly unlikely, he will still hang. He'll not lie about his relationship with her. That'll put the raw rope around his tender neck.

Back in my room I unseal the two photographs. He's standing with his grandmother. I know that without asking. He has his arm around her with his hand on her shoulder. She's uncomfortable with that small show of affection. He knows it. He's teasing her. She's annoyed. They're happy to be with each other. I turn to me and my grandmother. We're standing side-by-side. We're not touching. We're looking straight ahead. I'm uncomfortable around her. I would never, ever dare tease her.

Both grandmothers are bigger than they appear. They dominate the pictures if you look closely. Both old women ignore me. I'm beneath contempt to them. Fuck them. What can I do? His own words and deeds will hang him. Fuck them. I seal them in a new envelope. I hide the envelope in my book case.

###

Our second session is on life at Camp Oswald. Oswald was our most isolated post with two hundred troops and six Air lift troop-cargo copters and a small Cessna for forward observation. The Provincial Capital of Vimh, a town of several thousand, was less than ten miles from the Camp. The 9th Infantry company was there to "secure the Province against enemy incursion and to protect the inhabitants from coercion and exploitation by enemy forces." They carried out their missions with regular patrols and "quick air response to incidents of aggression." This is the purpose of Camp Oswald according to the US Army.

The Corporal has a different view of the Camp. He calls it "Happy Camp" because everyone was happy and high or drunk most of the time. Patrols did go out on a regular basis, but only to find a quiet, relatively safe, spot to get high or sleep off a previous high. The Happy Camp troops and the insurgents took great pains to avoid each other. Happy Camp casualties were low and mostly self-inflicted. The Happy Camp troops were very religious. They prayed to the insurgents to let them come back from each patrol and to let Happy Camp survive another day. Camp security was pretty much of a joke. Why pretend to be secure when there was no way in hell you could keep the enemy out or even tell who the enemy was most of the time?

If you weren't on patrol or some other assignment, you could leave the Camp pretty much at will, just be back in time for your next assignment. The rumor was that the insurgents were providing them with the high-quality weed, Green Witch. The Witch was ubiquitous. It was pretty much a live and let live arrangement until the Special Forces showed up and actually wanted to "kill some gooks."

I check it all out. I substantiate each and every one of his claims. The picture is worse than he presented. Happy Camp is place of despair where men have been abandoned to perform an impossible task. They are hopelessly outnumbered and outgunned by the enemy.

Happy Camp exists because the insurgents allow it to exist. Everyone knows Camp Oswald is a bad joke played on the men and officers assigned to the Camp.

###

I have lunch with Corporal Wilson every day. I bring the foods he likes. I pay for the food, but I feel like he's treating me. I want to hear about him and his grandmother. I want to know if she overpowered him, if she ruled the entire family with an iron fist. I always end up talking about me and my grandmother. After each visit I swear I'll not visit him again, but I do. I visit every day. I live for those visits. Am I falling in love with Corporal Wilson or is it something stronger than that?

###

And so the court martial commences. I do the best work of my life. I exceed even my own high opinion of myself. I get the desertion charge dismissed early on. Four other charges are dismissed over the next three days. The treason charge stands. The prosecution theory is that Wilson told Pham about the plans for a "secret" mass sweep of the northern three provinces enabling the enemy to strike at the optimal time and that by having intercourse during the attack on Camp Oswald, he gave substantial aid and comfort to the enemy. It's all bullshit. Bullshit that will leave Wilson dangling from a rope.

Tomorrow's the last day of the court martial. I'm amazed. I didn't think I would get any character witnesses for Wilson. I talked to thirteen men who served with him. To a man they're willing to testify on his behalf. Amazing. But he'll still hang.

I'm in the Colonel's office. It's nine PM. We're drinking scotch straight up. The Colonel is deep into his cups. "Captain, do you see it now? Do you understand political theater?"

I nod. "I'm out of moves sir. I... I... I'm sorry." I'm near collapse. This is the hardest I have fought for anything in my entire life.

The Colonel ignores me. "Political theater, we put those tiny little outposts up there so we can claim that we control the Northern Provinces. The American people see the map of our control. It looks like we control most of the damn country."

"Colonel, is there anything at all we can do now? Anything?"

The Colonel is lost in his world of political theater. "The insurgents play along. Once we claim the area is pacified, we find it difficult to justify major military actions in these areas or even reinforcements for our boys. The insurgents can move troops and material through at will. It would be suicide for an outpost to take on the insurgents, political theater."

Happy Camp fell so quickly, in part, because General Austen, the Commander of Northern Forces, had implemented a "secret" coordinated mass sweep of the three Northern Provinces, dispersing the troops from four camps and three bases. All these bases and camps fell within a seventy-two-hour period. The sweep was a crazy idea to start with. And it was far from secret. I have shown that in the court martial. It's not enough. I have established that Corporal Wilson did not know about the attacks at the time he had his last sexual encounter with Colonel Pham. It's not enough. He was fucking Colonel Tien Pham while his friends were dying. Tomorrow the court martial will end. The death watch will start. The colonel has passed out at his desk.

I stagger home. A small brown box is on my doorstep. I open it in my kitchen, pictures. I turn the box over and let the pictures fall to the table. I pick up a picture of General Austen. He's not alone. He's sharing his bed with a very nude very gorgeous Asian woman. I recognize her instantly as one of the beauties from the bar picture with Pham. I call the colonel. He tells me to ram that picture up their collective asses.

I get the Judge and the Prosecutor out of bed. We meet at the Judge's home. The pictures are examined with considerable intensity. Calls are made. Coffee is consumed. Calls are returned. More coffee is consumed. We wait for one call. It comes at six AM. Corporal Wilson will plead guilty to a lesser charge and do six years with a dishonorable discharge. I want to run to Wilson and give him the good news. I need to call the colonel, but first... As soon as I get to my quarters, I take the envelope out of the bookshelf. The grandmothers are still ignoring me. Fuck them! What more can I do? I toss the pictures on the floor and collapse onto my big living room chair.

I need to see a picture of Wilson and Pham together, now. I dream the picture. She's straddling his lap wearing a tight, short skirt. She's pulling down his zipper. He's ripping off her panties. This is not a show of affection... no... no... it's something else... lust... more... than lust... uncompromising need... I can smell them in heat... disorienting... I think; I have the absurd belief that the War, the whole War, was just an event to bring these two together. I awake suddenly with a sense of alarm. I race to the stockade. Wilson comes in the interview room looking very somber. I want to give him the good news. I want to give him, me. He doesn't want to listen or talk. He embraces me, thanks me and tells me to go home. He tells me everything will be all right. But he's not talking about himself. He's talking about me. There's nothing wrong with me. I'm safe. I'm almost sound.

The two grandmothers are smiling at me, at me. They look proud. I don't understand why or what happened. Still, I feel better than I can remember feeling in a long time. Something phenomenal has happened somewhere. Something epic and I have been part of it. I know that. I don't think saving Corporal Wilson's life is that event.

I sleep my best sleep in a long time. The last thing I remember is the musky odor of their love making.

Litter Wagon

I get a hop on a C-124 litter wagon. An empty plane except for me and the crew, dead-heading back to Dover AFB. Going home on leave, at last. Happy to be leaving Frozen Labrador. Glad to be headed to sunny California.

Old Shaky lives up to its name. The four props all seem to be vibrating at a different frequency. I say a prayer that this rickety old bumble bee is still air worthy. It is a double decked empty warehouse of rows and rows of litters. No seats. I'm the only passenger. I lie down on a stretcher and strap myself in. This old bird reeks of pain, suffering, grief, and despair. It is a hollow, ghostly feeling to be alone back here where the wounded and broken bodies of young men and boys take this flying ambulance home from Vietnam. I think I can smell the blood, piss, and vomit. I can feel the fever and pain deep in my bones.

The out-of-sync props make the old ship, moan, groan, shriek and cry. The faint stain on my litter is something I would rather not think about. Up, up and away to 12, 000' and home. God speed us.

Soon joined by a flight crew member asking about the duty-free liquor we radar site troops get. I'm glad to share my Crown Royal. Glad for the company

Soon after, joined by other crew members and both pilots, we huddle together on the upper deck, drinking and avoiding the mission of this beast. The pilots do not sit on the litters. They stand and drink, or sit on the deck.

We talk about anything but Vietnam.

Forty minutes out, alarms sound. The flight crew scatter to their stations. I strap myself in. They feather the right inboard engine and drop down to 8,000'. We pick up where we left off. Sometime later, more alarms. They feather the left inboard engine. We drop down to 4,000'.

The flight crew is confident we can get home on two engines and a continuous flow of Crown Royal. I'm not so sure.

The five of us finish off nearly a half-gallon of whiskey.

We walk off the plane at Dover, stone-cold sober. The flight crew heads for the nearest bar. I look for another hop home to California. Anything will do except another litter wagon. I would rather walk.

The Home Front

It was 1966. I was just four days out of the Air Force and staying with my cousin, Carolyn, in The District. Her high-rise projects were just a few blocks from the Capitol.

It was Monday morning, about 7:00. I was teaching Carolyn to drive my stick-shift sports car. She was trying to back out of the parking slot. I was headed back up to her apartment, to be with her boys when they woke up. The parking lot was deserted except for a few derelict cars.

The black-and-white rolls into the parking lot, like some animal on the prowl. I see it stop. The driver stares at the California plates on my car.

I keep moving toward the apartment building, holding my breath. I smell trouble, like sulfur, seeping out of the black and white.

There is a real stink in the air now.

"Hey, boy, is that your car?"

I'm 24 years old. I just did four years in the Air Force. I'm nobody's boy. I bite my tongue. I stop. I turn to face them.

"Yes, sir, that's my car."

I wait there close to the lobby doors.

The driver gets out of the car and beckons me toward him. He's a white man about my age. Looks a little like Kirk Douglas in a bad mood.

I take a deep breath and cross to him.

"You from California? Is that your car?"

I look him in the eyes. "My car, and we both from California."

The other cop gets out and moves around to my side, just out of my vision.

The other cop speaks: "You parked illegal. You on the line there."

The first cop adds his assent. "You need to move your car."

"Move it now," echoes the second cop."

I have been lucky. Carolyn has not jumped into this. Her temper is firecracker hot, and her language will take the paint off a barn at a hundred yards.

I step around the Kirk Douglas looking cop and slide over to my car. I lean in the car window.

"What the fuck do the shit eaters want? The fat ass mother-"

I cut her off.

"No matter what happens, you stay in this car. Understand me on this. The boys are upstairs. Remember that. Back out. Park the car in the back of the building and go in the back door and check on the boys."

"Fuck you Walter. We have to live with these lard ass, crooked, motherfuckers every day. I'll back over that ugly motherfucker. I-"

"Shut-up!" Wonder of wonders - she does. I show her how to find reverse, again. I step back and she slowly starts to back out.

I look up, and both cops are moving angrily toward me.

"Hey, boy I told you to move that fucking car!"

I meet them half way.

Carolyn stops the car. She steps out of the car, and all eyes turn to her. She is 25, light-skinned, cute, with a good figure and long hair.

I hold up my hand and stop her in mid stride.

I turn to the cops.

"My cousin or I will move the car, whatever you want."

It's too late for me. They think I'm showing them up with a fancy California car, and a good-looking woman. It's too much for them to take this early in the morning.

Kirk Douglas has gone all red in the face. The other cop has his night stick out. Better that than his gun.

"Turn around. Put your hands behind your back. Now! Do it now!" Kirk is practically screaming his orders at me.

I turn to Carolyn, "Please, please go upstairs now."

I lock eyes with her. I beg her. She starts toward the apartment with her face so tight I think it might break, and steps so stiff she is stabbing the ground.

I'm not complying fast enough for the cops. Nightstick cop moves in to bring me to my knees with his baton. Kirk Douglas is calling for backup.

A woman screams out a warning to me from her project window. "Watch out! He coming up behind you. Watch out."

Carolyn is at the lobby doors when she hears that warning. She spins around and charges the night stick cop. She is armed with teeth, nails, knees and elbows and incredible rage. She will hurt somebody or die trying.

Spencer, the project security guard, races over and wraps her up. He lifts her off her feet and hauls her back into the lobby. She is calling Spencer and the cops everything but a child of God.

I thank Spencer from the bottom of my heart as they cuff me. Another squad car screams into the parking lot, followed by a paddy wagon.

Six cops in all. I step up into the empty paddy wagon.

One cop asks another did they search me. One of them grabs the back of my sweater to pull me backward out of the paddy wagon.

I lean forward and fall into the paddy wagon on my face.

Someone grabs my leg and is pulling me out of the wagon. I roll over on my back. I see it's Kirk pulling me.

With my free foot, I kick him in the face as hard as I can. He falls back flat on his ass.

The rest is all a blur. They beat me there in the parking lot, all of them. They hit each other with their night sticks trying to get to me.

The project women save my life. They are screaming out the windows at the cops. They call the Capitol Police, The District police, the FBI and every other police agency in The District and the Fire Department and the press.

I get hauled away to a Precinct Station. They toss me in the drunk tank with the cuffs still on, and both eyes nearly swollen shut. I can't walk. I can barely stand.

Within minutes, Spencer and Carolyn are at the station asking for me.

The arresting cops whisk me away to another Precinct Station. The station cops tell her I'm not there.

Carolyn calls her ex-boyfriend, a DC cop. He finds me, still cuffed in another Precinct drunk tank.

They get me out within hours. I have no feelings in my hands.

I can't go back to the projects. Spencer tells Carolyn they will be waiting for me there.

Carolyn's ex says a hospital in The District is not a safe place for me.

I see our old family doctor in Falls Church.

The next day, five days out of the Air Force, I'm in Virginia buying a Browning automatic pistol. I never carried a gun in the service, but I will on the home front. I will carry it, and I will use it.

GAINFUL EMPLOYMENT

The Appointment

I'm up on the executive floor, all carpets and executive secretaries all in a row. Supplicants, anxious and eager, wait outside paneled doors, and then there's me, summoned from the bowels of the earth, to sit on this hot seat in the corner office with windows.

I'm one of four Civil Rights Coordinators. New pariah positions created to prevent discrimination in employment, and in the delivery of services within the California Department of Community Health Services.

Tidy White Girl, Executive Assistant, is sitting next to me trying to put as much distance between us as possible. She would prefer to be on the other side off the desk with the executive officer where she knows she belongs. The executive, ex-navy officer, well bred, slick dresser, thinks I'm his batman because I'm black, and not an officer, and nobody's boy. He's my direct supervisor who would rather not see me at all, or see me as a fuzzy face in a distant place. It galls him to even have to speak to me face to face, too low in the ranks to rate a face to face, face to ass, maybe, but even that might be pushing my luck."And how are you today? I apologize for the delay in meeting with you. We have been rather busy, a bit of a mess up here in fact. But better a little late, than never, right? I want to reassure you that we want Affirmative Action and civil rights to be part of our agenda, a very important part of our agenda."

Translation: "How I wish I never had to deal with you and your insignificant, absurd little job. The later the better and never is best. We will never have time, never for your silly civil rights and your regressive affirmative action. I just need you for a toilet paper mission I can flush, and you will not even be a memory."

I nod, don't smile. I Look at Tidy White Girl and then back at him.

Shit-eating grin. "Tidy should be here in case you need anything. Need to keep her up to speed you know."

Translation: "You want me to report to your Executive Assistant and leave you the fuck alone." Tidy is nervous at being in this awkward position. Too bad, this shit is probably going to get a lot worse.

Appointment paperwork for me to sign and sign now, it is my Declaration of Independence. They need my lowly signature because the boss bigger than his boss says that's the way the shit flows, uphill, for a change of pace. A silver pen there for my signature on the spot, on the dotted line, and I can return to my hole until next Groundhog's Day. They, both of them, are holding their breaths waiting for the nigger to jump through the hoop. Jump, nigger, jump. I admire the finely wrought silver pen.

"A critical appointment for the Department, the Director wants this completed today." Delivered with more than a touch of impatience.

"With such a high level appointment, I need to consult with the Civil Rights Officer. It would be unconscionable of me to approve an appointment at this level without his review and input." My shit-eating smile. Translation: "Fuck you, and the horse you rode in on, and fuck Tidy too."

Red-faced now barely holding on to his temper. "Is that really necessary? You have the authority to approve this. Right?" The question is directed to Tidy not me.

Tidy adds a blush to her arsenal of unease. "I think so, no, I mean yes he does."

"I does. I will make this my top priority." I smile sweetly at Tidy. "Page 12 of the AA Plan: 'The Civil Rights Coordinator will consult with the Department Civil Rights Office and other relevant authorities as necessary or prudent.' That's about the third paragraph I think."

I'm ushered out on a wave of anger from the Exec and little wavelet of anxiety from Tidy.

The Executive Secretaries know. They have a sixth sense about shit like this. That nigger is trouble. Watch him close. He might steal something or stab someone. He's not completely tame. Don't feed or pet him. Never let him out of your sight when he's up here.

###

I enter Alberto's office, and the Civil Rights Officer waves me to silence as he talks on the phone. "Yes…. Of course… ummhum… absolutely. Yes, yes…. No, no thank you." Alberto chuckles as he hangs up.

"Hey, my brother, that was The Man. He's very unhappy with you. Like, I think you may not be getting a Christmas card from him this year. If you do, it'll say, R.I.P."

I pull my chair close to his desk and prop my feet up on his desk. "Well, yeah, but I'll get a card from you, and that means sooo much more."

"I don't know, rookie. Look at it like this. The Man has promised me that office space we need and, and a manager slot in the Civil Rights Office. And you know who would look good in that manager slot?"

"Promises, promises, promises, it's a con, Alberto. Who you gona get to enforce those promises? Shit, he done already forgot that shit."

Alberto leans across the desk toward me. "Maybe. Maybe. But you got to sign anyway, right? So if you got to sign, we might as well get paid. Right, brother?"

"Bullshit. You start off trading away your integrity, and you'll be a joke in this Department and in State Service. You-

"Preston, integrity don't pay any bills. I can put you to work training investigators and keeping us up with the laws and regs, and you can work a nine-to-five job. Gloria-"

"Alberto, don't do this shit man, please."

"Or I could tell him you are a bit of a hot head, a militant and probably not the best fit for your current position, which requires finesse and an aaaww appreciation for the big picture."

I'm on my feet now. "Fuck you! And fuck you!-"

"Yeah, there goes that militant streak. A round peg in a square hole… too bad. Wake up Preston, these are Republican times even with that peanut farmer in the White House."

"Alberto, you don't even know militant, but I'm going to teach you."

Now, Alberto is on his feet. "You won't teach me shit. I have been in this business for five fucking years, and this is how it fucking works. You need to learn that, rookie. You need to learn it fast."

I'm patting my right foot rapidly. A clear sign I'm about do or say something I will regret. I take deep slow breaths. "If you're serious about this, and I believe you are, you should ask for thirty pieces of silver. The silver will go good with that yellow streak up your back."

"Get out of my office. Go home. Talk to Gloria. Come in tomorrow and we'll make this work for us. I promise. Hey, speaking of silver, if you got his fucking pen, you better give it back or lose it."

As I leave I give him my last thoughts on the appointment, "Make sure you take a big jar of Vaseline up there to collect your fucking filthy coins. You're going to need it, but I'm sure you know that by now. Five years of bending over… you probably keep a keg of Vaseline in here."

I'm sick to my stomach. Alberto and I have been friends for over a decade. I walk my lunch hour away. I don't eat. What a long fucking day this is. Will it ever end?

Heidi, of the too tight blouse and the too short skirt, and the too red, red lipstick, is worried and pacing my little office. "Preston, you have to think about this. Think about this carefully now. You can't win, you know that."

I'm sipping tea and admiring her long, long legs and wondering how long I will have that view and this office. "Yeah, Alberto already told me that. Now, get back out front. We have a full schedule this afternoon. We got work to do woman. Move your ass."

At the office door, she turns back to me. "Preston this is the best job ever. I love it. And I really thank you for it, but if you fuck this up, I will never forgive you, never." She's almost out the door when she turns back. "The Exec sent his prissy little Executive Assistant down here looking for a silver pen. Do-"

"Go to work, Heidi. We got no time for that nonsense."

Heidi is a fallen angel. She was an Executive Secretary up on the executive floor, but she played a little too hard and somebody's wife complained to the Director, and she has been cast down into our limbo. She still gets Executive Secretary pay, but she does receptionist duty and typing for my office and two other programs.

I supervise her. I'm giving her analyst duties, and she's a natural and a first-rate secretary. My wife's not real happy with Heidi as my secretary/analyst. She has had a little chat with Heidi and a very serious talk with me, all completely unnecessary of course.

Heidi still has friends on the executive floor, and at 4:45PM they alert her that Tidy is on her way down to collect the signed appointment papers. As part of my job, I investigate discrimination complaints. Almost every day I come in early and leave late. Today I'm interviewing complainants until 5:40PM. A very anxious Tidy is waiting outside my office. Her orders are, if I do not give her the signed papers, she's to escort me up to see the Exec who also works late. It's wonderful how the Exec, and I have so much in common.

###

He's at the very edge of ballistic. I show him the appointment history for the class he's seeking to make an appointment to. There are currently no blacks, women, Hispanics, Asians, or disabled, in this civil-service classification and as far as I can tell, there never have been. The appointment he's seeking to make is a white male. We have only seven positions in this Department, of over 4,000 employees, in this classification. All of them are white males.

He's not impressed. He wants a signature now. Right now.

I tell him I'm eager to sign, but this gross disparity, coupled with our failure to advertise the position to give others a chance to apply, has deeply disturbed me, and at this point, I'm leaning strongly toward recommending rejecting the appointment.

He goes ballistic, impressively so. Tidy shrinks to about two inches tall. The curtains in his office are moving as if in a strong breeze and the papers on his desk jump with each pounding of his fist.

I enjoy the show. When he finally winds down, I tell him that the Civil Rights Officer, in his great wisdom, has suggested rather than reject the appointment, I sleep on it and make a decision in the morning.

The Exec appears to be having some problem breathing. I step forward to offer my assistance, but he waves me out of his office. I know how to take a hint. Besides I have some serious deliberations to start.

"You'll sign in the morning. You need to stop playing games. You love your job, and you're good at it."

She is washing dishes, and I'm drying them and putting them away. We have a dishwasher, but we like sharing household chores.

Babe, right now, this very minute, I would not sign. And as to Alberto, fuck him. What an asshole."

She stops washing dishes and turns to face me. "Look, I think you better look at where you are, and who you're working with. It will be awful to have no one on your side. That could be very difficult, Preston."

"Gloria, babe, Alberto is trading favors for stuff he has a right to. Personnel has approved the manager position and with that comes more office space. The Exec is just offering him what he has a right to."

"Preston, you know having positions approved, and actually getting the positions, are very different propositions-"

"Fuck, the reason we set up the Affirmative Action system is to give everyone a fairer shot at openings. And now we trade other employees' opportunities for our own personal gain. That's bullshit!"

Aww shit we're locked into an argument. An argument I don't need or want. "Preston, Preston, you are so stubborn sometimes just, just ... think about it, OK? Whatever, you do. I'm with you, honey. You know that."

"Stubborn is good sometimes. That's how I got you. I must have asked you out what, twenty times?"

"Five times, and you didn't get me. I got you. You chased me until I caught you."

"No, you were dating-"

"I was toying with you. Playing you like a piano."

"Really?"

"Yes, really."

"Are you playing me now?"

She giggles, and I pull her into my arms. She comes willingly.

"Babe, you know that was a fight, right? And you know what that means."

She looks puzzled. "Whatever are you talking about, dear sir?"

We have make-up sex. We have it on the way to and in the bedroom.

I'll never understand Gloria. We have been married for three years. They have been the best three years of my life. She still surprises me in unexpected and wonderful ways. In the morning, she reminds me again that I wrote most of the Affirmative Action plan, and that I worked hard to set up the AA system.

"Don't throw it all away on this battle. You're going to win the war, baby. I know it. And, you did good by Heidi if - and if - you make a deal, you could get her an analyst position."

"But, but you came to the office and talked to Heidi. I thought-"

"You did right by Heidi. You could have taken advantage of her or rejected her. She was crushed by what happened to her. You gave her real work and respect. I'm proud of you for that."

"So what did you two talk about?"

"I just told her I thought what had happened to her was unfair, and that you were a good man and a good supervisor."

"I thought- So, what was all that shit you gave me about keeping my dick in my pants. What was that all about?"

"Oh, that's always a timely subject for your gender. Your dicks are always leading you into trouble."

"You didn't say that last night. You said- "She shuts me up with a kiss. I glance at the clock. I think we have time…

###

At 7:30AM, I already have an employee waiting in my office and another surprise.

Heidi is dressed in a plain, loose white blouse with only one button undone and black, not too tight, below the knee skirt, and simple flat black shoes.

"Heidi, would you step into my office for just a moment."

"What are you doing? Why are you dressed like that?"

"It's office appropriate attire and it's what you want me to dress like."

"I never said anything about how-"

"I know, but this is better for-"

"Heidi, I'm going to sign. I'm going to approve the appointment. Please dress the way you like, OK?"

"You're going to sign? You're going to approve it?" She's practically jumping with joy. She kisses me on the cheek as she leaves the office.

###

The call comes in at 8:05AM. It's from Audrey Tanaka, the Senior Executive Secretary, who's in charge of all the executive secretaries. We have never spoken to each other. She tells me they are plotting to use a problem in my promotion paperwork to say I'm not qualified for my current position. They will appoint Tidy White Girl to my position until the paperwork problem is corrected, and she'll approve the appointment. The Exec was working on this even as he was promising Alberto the moon, sun and stars. She's telling me this because I helped her daughter-in-law out of a very oppressive situation in our San Francisco Field Office. I hang up the phone. I call Alberto and explain what's happening.

"That double crossing son-of-a-bitch. Fuck em all to hell. Hold on, Preston. I'll get back to you."

He calls his girlfriend at Agency, the Department that oversees our Department.

Twenty minutes later, he calls me back and reads me the Memo that's on its way to our Director. The Memo says that, effective immediately, appointment paperwork submitted without the signature of an Agency Approved Civil Rights Coordinator, will be rejected. The Memo lists the four Civil Rights Coordinators in our Department. My name is first on that list.

I get another surprise ten minutes later. Tidy is in my office. She's near tears. She tells me about the promotion paper work scam. She's going to resign her position. She wants no part of that dirty trick.

I tell Tidy, or Pam, her name is Pamela Schmidt, to keep her job. Everything will be fine. She doesn't believe me, but she promises to hold off on her resignation until the end of the day.

At 9:30AM, Pam and I are in the Exec's office. He has received the Agency Memo. He's sullen and angry. He bites off his few bitter words.

I stand over his desk and sign the paperwork with his pen. I pause over the recommendation boxes, and I check the "Rejection" box. I can't help it. I toss the pen on his desk.

They strike back. The Director calls me in after lunch. In his spacious office, there are only the Director, the Exec, and me. The Director does not offer me a seat.

"It has come to my attention, through a variety of sources, that you may be engaged in an affair with Heidi Marsh, and you well know that such an affair is in violation of Department rules and regulations. Pending an investigation into these allegations, you will be reassigned to an Audit unit in Folsom. One of the other Civil Rights Coordinators will take over your case load."

His final words are: "Mrs. Tanaka and several others have spoken out on your behalf. For their sakes and yours, I hope the allegations are proven unfounded." To me, it sounds like he's saying that when I'm found guilty, my foolish supporters will also lose their heads.

Morales promises to look out for Heidi. Gloria is supportive in every way.

Folsom is Governor Moonbeam's Gulag Archipelago where all the outsiders, malcontents and whistle blowers are sent to wind down their careers. The first familiar face I see is Tidy White Girl. We both agree that this is a minor career setback, and our respective spouses and friends love and support us to the fullest. So, why are we fucking like minks in the backseat of Pam's car during our lunch hour?

The Hearing

"So, Mr. Samuel Wilson, you have no trial experience. Did you do Moot Court in law school, or an internship that allowed you to participate in, or witness trials, or administrative hearings?"

My interrogator, Lena Morgan, is the Office Administrator for the Legal Division of the Department of Adult and Child Care. She is a heavyset, no-nonsense woman, with only traces of blond in her gray hair.

"No, no Ma'am. I have represented employees at administrative hearings, but never as an attorney."

She seems slightly perplexed by my lack of trial experience. She studies me for a minute, looks me in the eyes, and leans toward me over her cluttered desk. "Well, you are the first virgin I have seen here in fifteen years. The work we do here demands experience. You have to hit the ground running."

I lean in and smile back at her. "I have on my running shoes. I can play catch-up."

"Humm ... we are going to see about that, aren't we? You will need a strong experienced Secretary and Legal Analyst to help you. And I have a pair that would be perfect for you, but Maria Gonzales, the Legal Secretary, is going on maternity leave this week. And Gabby Salazar, the Analyst, is tied up with a major case." Morgan studies me for a moment, and drums her fingers on her desk. "We have the three other new attorneys going through our regular three-week training, but that is for experienced attorneys. Not a good place for you to start, so, what are we to do with you?"

"I'm willing to run with the big dogs. I think I can keep up-"

"Wilson, are you willing to take a gamble, a leap of faith, say, and work with ahh, ahh, a different personality, but very knowledgeable?"

Now, I sit back and take in Morgan's office littered with boxes, case files, stacks of printouts, and scattered law books. She is comfortable with my taking my time and scoping out her den. She is comfortable with getting old, letting her grey hair show. I decide I trust her. I like her.

"Different, humm, sounds like difficult might be a better word... but I want to trust your judgment. Can I do that?" Morgan chuckles, "Yeah. I think you just might work. We will try it for a few days and see how it goes. Now, this is critical, if you feel ... aaahh ... overwhelmed, or just real uncomfortable, come see me immediately. You got that?"

"Is this Attila the Hun, or Ted Bundy you're fixing me up with?"

Now she laughs loud and clear, "You should be so lucky, Samuel. Can I call you Samuel?"

"Sure, but-"

"Listen her bite is way worse than her bark. If she finds she can dominate you, she will. She has left one of our star attorneys in tears and forced another to leave the Department. She can be more than a handful."

Now, I'm starting to get a little worried. This is my first job as an attorney. I'm forty years old, and I struggled to get this damn degree and pass the Bar. My wife and kids put up with a lot to help me get here. I don't want to blow it all on my first job. Still, a baptism by fire... shit... I did that in Nam... I think I'm going to trust Morgan this once.

Morgan has summoned my Legal Analyst/Legal Secretary/trainer. Her name is Anna Kemper. Morgan and I exchange small talk while we wait for this hell on wheels, lawyer devouring, fire breathing dragon, that is going to help me catch up with the seasoned troops.

Morgan has just warned me not to be shocked by Anna's appearance just as the dragon darts into her office like an angry bee.

I can't help it. I stare. I blink. My jaw drops. She stands in front of Morgan's desk with her petite hands on her miniature hips and a frown on her angry little face. She is clearly pissed, all 4' 8" or so of her. She is tiny, tiny, with gold hair and almond-shaped sparkling blue eyes, and a little upturned nose. She is a dead ringer for Tinkerbelle. I mean, her hair is in a bob, and she is wearing short heels, a white blouse and blue skirt, but even with that, she is the spitting image of Tinkerbelle. My first thought is to paste some wings on her, and take her home for my girls, eight and nine, to play with. I have to try really hard not to break out in a fit of uncontrollable laughter.

Morgan confronts Kemper before the fairy can cast a spell or sprinkle pixie dust.

"Not a word, Kemper. Not one word. You are on my shit list, at the very top of my list. So, meet Samuel Wilson, your new attorney to train and explain life hereabouts."

She spins to look at me, looks me up and down and those blue eyes are chips of jagged blue marble. Not very friendly or Disney like at all.

She turns back to Morgan. The little elf finally speaks, "Why me? Is he mentally challenged or brain damaged?" Her voice is not tiny at all. It carries weight. Authority. Anger. Not a voice you can ignore or laugh at. I'm starting to regret my decision to work with this imp.

"I'm beginning to think I'm a little of both." I offer her my hand. She crosses her arms under her breast and sneers at me. The little snot actually sneers at me.

Morgan intervenes. "Dial it down Kemper. You two make a lovely couple. Off you go now, and don't forget to write."

At that moment, I'm starting my own shit list and Morgan, and Kemper are at the top.

###

"Are you telling me you have no real or imagined court room experience? I will kill Morgan. No, that's too easy. She will die the death of a thousand paper cuts, the old cow. And you - you could have told me before I got into this situation."

I'm sitting in a chair in her impossibly neat office as she paces back and forth in front of me.

"I live in Southgate. I drive by the court house every day, and I used to watch Perry Mason, if that helps."

She is not at all impressed with my sense of humor. "Have you ever written an accusation?"

"No, but I have been accused of lots of stuff. I have been accused of so many-"

"Shut up."
And that's how I started my apprenticeship with Captain Bligh.

I'm working in the small conference room across from her office. I have a cubicle office, but she says I need to concentrate free of interruptions. I have three accusations drafted by different Department attorneys. I have the case files including the decisions. My job is to do a critical analysis of the three, five, and ten page documents, and rewrite the charges to make them more effective. I have three hours.

She rips my work to shreds. She finds problems that I missed in every document. She rewrites every one of my corrections, and I have to admit; her rewrites are vast improvements. Her contempt is palpable. It is more of the same after lunch. I think I will get at least one rewritten charge through her, but she crosses out my rewrite altogether as redundant, she's right. I have homework, five accusations to review.

"It's ten o'clock, babe, are you going to be much longer?"

I yawn, stretch and reach for my wife. She stays just out of my reach.

"You didn't work this hard in law school, last chance, going once, going twice…" She moves off toward our bedroom.

I'm truly beginning to hate fairies.

###

She reviews my homework, marks it up, and notes that at this rate, I will be sixty before I can write a decent accusation. Today I go back over the same accusations to look at compliance with our regulations, whether the citations are correct, and whether the correct regulation is cited. Again, I'm to correct any errors I find. I'm marginally better at this task, but the grim little elf is not impressed. Next, I go over the same documents to see if the regulations are a fair reflection of the laws they are based on. It is tedious, exacting, work, under a harsh, relentless little tyrant.

After lunch she summons Ailene Watson, one of the Senior Attorneys, into the meeting room. Ailene is the author of one of the truly dismal accusations that I have read. It was three pages of too vague or too specific or misapplied regulations.

"Kemper, what the hell is this? I'm on my way to LA. I don't have time for your shit today."

The little sprite turns to me, "Wilson. This is your instructor for as long as you find her helpful. She's going to explain how her accusation in the Bradley case cost us the case and gave the Department a long, lingering black eye."

"You horrid little bitch! You, you are so full of shit! I will... Fuck you!"

Watson starts out the door.

"Wilson's a virgin. He's never done a trial or an administrative hearing. The Chief Counsel hired him because the Director asked him to. I will personally inform the Director that you refused to assist in the training of his baby attorney. You should use your time in L.A. to look for a new job because you will be finished in this Department."

Watson is frozen with her hand on the door knob. She is shaking with rage and frustration. She turns to face me. She avoids looking at Kemper. She tells a short, bitter story of her legal analyst suddenly taking ill and another legal analyst from a different shop completing the accusation. Watson assumed the accusation was done by her very competent legal analyst and approved it without reviewing it. At the hearing, the judge would not allow the accusation to be amended or withdrawn because the hearing date was past due. The other side challenged the competence of the accusations. The judge found for the defendants. The recitation has taken a visible toll on Watson. Her complexion is pale, and her face is drawn. Her hands grip the back of the chair so hard I hear a finger nail snap. She just stares at me, waiting.

"A child had died in the facility. Surely the DA-"

She cuts me off. "The DA found no evidence of criminal liability in the death." Now, she hates me as much as she hates Kemper. "Is that all? I have to catch a flight."

"Just, when did you discover the accusation was screwed up?"

She spits out, "At the hearing. I have to go now."

I nod for her to go.

Watson slumps out like a broken rag doll.

I catch immediate hell from the very angry elf.

"That was a learning opportunity Wilson. It cost her a lot to be here. I will pay hell for that expensive lesson, and you have two softball questions. Do you even want to work here?"

"You didn't have to do that. There are better ways to teach that lesson."

"Teach what lesson? What lesson did you learn?"

"Treating people with respect is a lesson I learned early on."

"Really? But you're a long way from learning to be an effective attorney."

"Kemper, she made a mistake. We all make mistakes, even you."

"Mistakes! You think this is about mistakes? That slime ball is still here drawing Senior Attorney salary. If you cared about respect, if you had even a little bit of attorney in you, you would have asked what happened to her legal analyst."

"The analyst fucked up. Even I saw that when I first looked at the accusation."

"No, you are wrong again. The analyst who drafted the accusation came from the policy shop. She had never drafted an accusation. She wasn't familiar with the regs. She was told to put something in the computer system as a place holder that the attorney would complete. She had thirty minutes to enter something."

"I, I didn't know-"

"That analyst is gone. She received most of the blame when Bradley went south. Shit rolls downhill."

"Look, I didn't-"

"You didn't ask. You didn't ask the right questions. Watson's regular analyst was invited not to return to the Department after her gall stone surgery. Both gone, Watson's still here." All of sudden Kemper looks tired like her little internal light bulb had dimmed. "Wilson, take the rest of the day and do what you will. You report to Morgan in the morning. She doesn't spring away as usual. She seems to fade out of the room.

###

"What an interesting work place you have. Kemper sounds like she is on a vendetta. You may be better off joining the training with the other new attorneys."

Cindy and I are cuddling on our couch having a glass of wine after finally getting our girls to sleep. "I don't know. She's a damn good trainer and knowledgeable... smart... I don't know."

"Well, Mr. Wilson, it's not a matter of what you know. She sounds like she has cut you lose."

"Well, Mrs. Wilson, you may be right, and the other new attorneys do not have homework. That means I would have time to…"

"To help with the girls and to fix the vacuum cleaner, the lawn mower and-"

"Honey, a kiss is worth a thousand words."

I try to get a dictionary's worth of kisses.

###

"Good morning."

Kemper looks up from the case she's reading. "This is not Morgan's office."

I take a deep breath. "I want you to train me if you will. I need your help. You have helped me enormously, but I need more. I know I need a lot more."

She doesn't hesitate. She points to a thick case file on the edge of her desk. "Review it, every page of it. Know it. After lunch, you have a witness prep interview with Denise Means. Patterson has this case, but she has a hearing today. You will prep the witness and be at the hearing tomorrow to support Patterson. Go read."

I have a ton of questions, like why did she change her mind and how did she know I would be coming back to her. But, she's back reading her case.

"Who is Denise Means?" Kemper is at work even when she is driving and obviously enjoying her three series BMW convertible. She handles the BMW with ease and confidence in the downtown traffic and on the freeway.

"She is a six-year-old black girl who has been in county institutions and foster homes since the age of three. She is thin, undersized, has a slight lisp and is good at math. She has bad hair and an unhealthy charcoal colored skin. She collects bottle tops and loves to read." I pause as I recall the case file. "She is ... she is, a very strong little girl. She hasn't given up."

"Given up on what?"

I take so long to respond that Kemper glances over at me. "She hasn't given up on herself... she believes in herself and that things will get better. That's her religion, her lifeline."

"Wilson, I read that case file three times. I didn't see any evidence of her strength or optimism. What's bad hair?"

"It's in there. In her case - short, nappy hair that will not grow more than a couple of inches long."

Denise greets us at the door in a blue and white school uniform. Her foster mother, a very tall, homely looking white woman, is right behind her.

Denise is stunned when she sees Kemper. Her mouth drops open, she points at Kemper, and turns back to look at her foster mother while she continues to point at Kemper. The foster mother stops short, puts her hands to her chest and mutters, "Oh my, oh my."

Kemper puts on her icy, still as death voice. "Is there something you want to ask me?" The voice and the look on her face dispel any image of Tinkerbelle those two had formed.

Denise and her foster mother both are shaking their heads no and are trying desperately to look away from Tinkerbelle, I mean, Kemper.

Kemper, Denise, and I conduct the interview in Denise's bedroom. Kemper makes herself invisible speed-reading case files. The only other words Kemper, says during the entire visit are "Good bye." and "Thank you."

"Mr. Wilson is it hard to be a Lawyer? Are you rich? All lawyers are rich, Right? Do you have kids? Do they have a dog? Is that your car? It's pretty. We have food. I can open the fridge whenever I want. I'll show you." When she's finally over the initial gush of questions and comments, I answer each of her questions in the order she asked them. She keeps trying to sneak peeks at Kemper, but there is freeze zone around Kemper that discourages us from even looking in Kemper's direction.

I had planned to convince Denise to testify by telling her she would be protecting other kids, and that it was the right thing to do and that it was a demonstration of her bravery. I did none of that. I just talked to her about things she wanted to talk about. We looked at pictures of my daughters. "Wow, they are so pretty. Their mothers' pretty, huh?"

I admire her bottle top collection, "These are amazing. You must have drunk a lot of beer to get all these beer bottle tops."

The fifteen-year-old son of a previous foster mother had come into her bedroom when she was five and tried to force his dick into her mouth. She tried to fight, but he was two strong. She cried, and her roommate in the upper bunk screamed at the boy to stop that. She would do it. She did what the boy wanted, and her roommate pleaded with Denise not to tell anyone because it would just make things worse. The roommate was six years old. The boy came back two nights later and forced both of them to perform oral sex on him. This time Denise told her foster mother what happened. The foster mother slapped her, called her a liar. Denise called her social worker three times each day for the next three days and left messages with each call. Denise never got a response to her messages. The boy came back to her and her roommate twice during that period. One of the other foster kids told a different social worker what was happening to Denise and her roommate. It still took two weeks to move Denise and her roommate. The only reason the rapes stopped was because the boy was arrested on unrelated charges two days after the second social worker was informed of the assaults. She tells me the whole story and answers all my questions. She is quiet, still and remote as she talks about the events. It has taken eleven months for our Department to get the case to hearing.

I explain the hearing process and answer her questions. I ask her if she will testify.

"Will you be there?"

"Yes, but another attorney will be asking you the questions. She's very nice and very good at interviewing young people."

She thinks about it for a while. "You promise to be there?"

"I do." We shake on it.

She takes us for a tour of her home, shows me the fridge and the back yard and introduces me to the two other foster kids.

We drive back to the office. I don't have much to say, and Kemper has nothing to say until we park.

"She's your witness tomorrow. I will clear it with Patterson. You be ready."

She pauses for a minute and adds, "She is a very strong girl. I'm glad you saw that in the file."

###

Cindy and I are fixing dinner. The girls are doing homework.

"Well that was quick. I thought you were struggling with your little pixie, and now you are putting on a witness. What happened?"

"I'm not sure. I must have done all right in the witness prep."

The girls want to come to the hearing and see their dad in action. I tell them next time when I have my own case. Cindy wants to come to until I tell her about the case. She decides to pass on this hearing.

I don't worry about the hearing that night. I can't stop seeing Denise Means and her bottle top collection.

###

I arrive at the hearing room early. I have two legal pads of questions for Denise.

Kemper asks politely if she can see them. I hand the questions to her, and she pretends to read as she walks to the nearest trash bin and dumps my five hours of work into the bin. The little devil walks back to me and has the nerve to smile at me.

"Just do what you did yesterday. You will not have any problems with Denise."

She doesn't know how close she came to following those pads into that bin.

Abby Patterson is an attractive brunet in her mid-forties. She has a kind face, but she has a reputation for being a shark in the administrative hearings. She thanks me for putting on Denise. She gives me a few tips. I will be sitting at the prosecution table with her.

When Denise arrives, I spend ten minutes talking to her. She is delighted that I will be "her" attorney. She hugs me.

On the stand, I take Denise through the qualifying questions to establish her ability recall and relate factual information from the time of the alleged incidents. I establish that she knows the difference between the truth and a lie. I have her promise to tell the truth.

Judge Sampson finds her to be a competent witness. I make a motion to have Denise testify in a narrative fashion. The motion is not opposed by the defense attorney and is granted by the judge.

It was a rehash of my interview yesterday.

The cross-examination is effective and fair. I make only a few objections during cross, and I couch them as suggestions. The judge and the defense attorney go along with this approach.

I have a very short re-direct.

Patterson thanks me and compliments me on my court room manner and the effectiveness of my work.

Afterward, Kemper and I take Denise to lunch at McDonald's.

"The little thief stole your heart didn't she?"

Kemper and I are walking out of the garage and back to work after the hearing.

"What?"

"You want to adopter her and have her be part of your nice little middle-class life right?"

"Kemper you-"

"It won't work. Your girls will hate her, and your wife will not accept her, and she will be worse off than she is now."

"You presumptuous little bitch. You, you- did you ever think about plastic surgery and dying your hair black and wearing heels?"

"No. Did you ever think about bleaching your skin white and straightening your hair?"

I'm ashamed of what I just said. I can't look Kemper in the face.

"Well, I hope you got that out of your system. Come on, you have accusation drafting this afternoon."

"Did you apologize to her?"

"Cindy, I tried. What an asshole thing to say."

"Well, she got you back. You need to move on."

The next morning before I'm in the office good I'm told Morgan wants to see me ASAP.

Morgan's not in a good mood.

"Close the damn door. Sit!"

I sit. I start to explain about my comments to Kemper, but Morgan cuts me off.

"What did you do to Kemper? I have tried to be fair to you Wilson, and you go pull some shit like this."

I try to stammer out a response, but Morgan rushes on.

"Are you playing in the pixie dust? Are you lifting little fairy skirts?"

It takes me a moment to understand what Morgan is saying.

"What? What the hell are you talking about? Are you-"

"OK, OK sit back down. I just had to ask. I, I have known Kemper for years, and she has never raved about anyone like she did about you."

"Morgan, what the hell is going on here? Have you gone crazy?"

Morgan points to three large ugly looking case files on the front of her desk.

"That is the H. Williams case, a dog of a case involving two four-year-old victims. The case is an embarrassment to the Department. It is overdue. No one wants this case. Patterson was going to get this case because she's the best we have at working with children that young."

"OK, but what does this have to do with me and me having sex with Kemper?"

"Kemper said you were the best attorney in the Department to handle this case. She praised you, said you were 'a natural.' Kemper and praise are not a normal state."

"And, you jumped to the conclusion-"

"I have a dirty mind, so shoot me. Anyway, I checked with Patterson and lo and behold after some reflection she agreed with Kemper."

"I could have been sleeping with her also. Did you think about that?"

"OK, OK I apologize again. However, I never trust lawyers, especially, when they will dodge a bullet like the Williams case. So, I put my ear to the street, and the street told me that at least one judge thinks you could pull it off."

"Yeah, I could have been sleeping with her too."

"Knock it off. You got all the apology you are going to get. I can't force you to take this case. This is a case for a Senior Attorney, but, but if you take this case, you will not lack for any support or assistance that the Department can provide. This comes from the Director himself."

"What did Kemper say about me exactly?"

"Humm, 'He's not that bad'... and 'I've seen worse...' and 'better than average.' I think that about sums it up."

"Ohhh, huh, well aahhh ... if she thinks I can do it."

"Excellent, Wilson I can get you any help you will need."

"I don't think I'll need much help. Kemper's all the help I'll need."

"Wonderful, but she returns to the AG's office at the end of the week, two days from now."

"What? She never said anything about leaving."

"Yeah, well our little fairy got into it with the Chief Counsel over the fallout from the Bradley case, a very ugly scene, so she goes back. Don't feel sorry for her. She goes back with a promotion and she kind of created her own job over there."

Things are beginning to fall into place for me.

"Listen, you are not expected to win this case, just do your best and move it off the books. Patterson will co-chair if you want. Anything you want, anything you need, OK?"

###

We take a long lunch, and she has the top down as she puts the BMW through its paces on the South River roads' twist and turns. The sun is kind. The wind is gentle, and the little Beamer is purring with contentment.

"Wilson, what you have that makes you connect with the kids will kill you in this job. One year, eighteen months at the most and you find something else to do after that."

"I'm taking Denise and her foster sibling's roller skating after school on Thursday."

"I revise my advice, twelve months or less."

"Yes mother. I hear you. Can I call you if I need your help with the Williams hearing?"

"Are you going through the motions or are you serious about revoking the group home owner's license?"

She has on large dark glasses that cover her eyes and half her face. She looks straight ahead and takes the thirty mile per an hour curve at fifty.

"Wilson, the owner is a substantial corporation. You will be confronting first class legal talent, the best that money can buy."

She drops into second and screams by a truck doing forty.

"When it starts to get expensive, and it will; the Department will 'encourage' you to settle at any cost."

We slow to twenty-five as we enter the village of Sinclair.

"Are you prepared for the enemy to be the Department and Morgan?"

We leave Sinclair and are cruising at sixty-five.

"Kemper, the proof of the pudding is in the eating. You should come to the hearing and see for yourself what I do."

She does.

About the Author

Frederick K. Foote, Jr. was born in Sacramento, California and educated in a racially segregated elementary school in Vienna Virginia until he was twelve and returned to Sacramento and its economically and racially segregated schools. He served three years nine months in the USAF and retired from the State of California in 2001. Frederick taught at California Community colleges for over ten years and at a traditionally black college in South Carolina. He has been married for 46 years and has two daughters.